MW00325920

Gluten-Free Murder

Also by this Author

Gluten-Free Murder

Auntie Clem's Bakery
Book 1

P.D. Workman

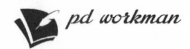

Copyright © 2017 P.D. Workman

All rights reserved. No part of this publication may be reproduced, stored in retrieval system, copied in any form or by any means, electronic, mechanical, photocopying, recording or otherwise transmitted without written permission from the publisher. You must not circulate this book in any format.

ISBN: 9781988390819

For nurturers everywhere,
feeding our souls as well as our bodies

Chapter One

ERIN PRICE PULLED UP in front of the shop and shut off her loudly-knocking engine. She took a few deep breaths and stared at the street-side view. She hadn't seen it since her childhood, but it looked just the same as she remembered it. Maybe a little smaller and shabbier, like most of the things from her childhood that she re-encountered, but still the same shop.

Main Street of Bald Eagle Falls was lined with red brick buildings, pasted shoulder-to-shoulder to each other, in varying, incongruous styles. Each one had a roofed-in front sidewalk to protect shoppers and diners from the blazing Tennessee sun they would face in the coming summer. All different colors. Some of them lined with gingerbread edges or whimsical paint jobs. Or both. Some of the stores appeared to have residences on the second floor, white lacy curtains drawn in windows that looked down at the vehicles, mostly trucks, nose-in in the parking spaces. There was no residence above Clementine's shop. She had lived in a small house a few blocks away that Erin had no memory of. She had spent most of her time at the shop and did not remember sleeping over at her aunt's when her parents had brought her for a visit.

A US flag hung proudly on a flagpole in front of the stores, just fluttering slightly in the breeze. It was starting to get dark and she knew she'd have to find the house in the dark if she were going to stop and take the time to explore the shop.

With another calming breath, Erin unbuckled her seatbelt, unlocked the door, and levered herself out of the seat. She felt like she'd been pasted into the bucket seat of the Challenger for three days straight. She *had* been pasted into the bucket seat for three days straight, other than pit-stops and layovers. She wasn't tall, so she wasn't crammed into the small car, but she'd been in there long enough to want to get out and straighten her body and stretch her legs. And to go to bed, but bed was still a long way off.

Erin walked up to the shop and put her key into the lock. It ground a little, like it hadn't been used for a long time. Maybe it needed a little bit of lubrication to loosen it up.

The air inside the shop was too still and too warm. She remembered when the little shop had been filled with the smells of exotic teas and fresh-baked goods, but Clementine had retired and closed it years ago. It had been a long time since anything had been baked there. It just smelled like dust and stale air. Erin left the front door open to let some fresh air circulate while she took a look around. There wasn't much space to explore in front of the counter. She would need a couple little tables, with a limited number of chairs, for the few people who wanted to eat in. Most of her business would just be stopping in to pick up their orders. She walked behind the counter. Everything seemed to be in good shape. A good wipe-down and some fresh baked goods in the display case and she'd be ready to go. Maybe a fresh coat of paint on the wall and a chalk board listing the daily specials and prices.

She walked into the back. A kitchen with little storage and a microscopic office that might once have been a closet. The back stairs led to a larger storage area downstairs, she remembered. And what Clementine had always called the commode. There was a second set of stairs from the store front down to the commode for customers. Not exactly convenient, but it was a small, old building. The arrangement had worked okay for Clementine. As a girl, Erin had always been a little afraid of the basement. She would creep down the stairs to use the bathroom and then race back up again, always drawing a warning from Clementine to slow down or she would trip and catch her death on those stairs.

All the old appliances were still there in the kitchen. Even a decades-old industrial fridge stood unplugged and propped open. There was no microwave and Erin was going to need a fancier coffee machine, but everything else looked usable.

"What are you doing here?"

Erin turned around and saw a looming figure in the kitchen doorway at the same time as the clipped male voice interrupted her thoughts. She just about jumped out of her skin.

She put her hand on her thumping chest and breathed out a sigh of relief when she saw that it was a uniformed police officer. But he wasn't looking terribly welcoming, jaw tight and one hand on his sidearm. There was a German Shepherd at his side.

"Oh, you scared me. I'm Erin Price," she introduced herself, reaching out her hand and stepping toward him, "and I'm—"

"I asked you what you're doing here."

Erin stopped. He made no move to close the distance between them and shake her hand, but remained standing there in a closed, authoritative stance. His tone brooked no nonsense. Erin couldn't imagine that she looked anything like a burglar. A little rumpled from the car, maybe, but she hadn't been sleeping in it. Was a slim, white, young woman really the profile of a burglar in Bald Eagle Falls?

"I own this shop."

He raised an eyebrow in disbelief, but he did let his hand slide away from the weapon and adopted a more casual stance. Erin allowed herself just one instant to admire his fit physique and his face. He was roguish, with what was either heavy five o'clock shadow or three days' growth, but his face was also round, giving him an aura of boyishness and charm.

"You own the shop. And you are…?"

"Erin Price. Clementine's niece."

"If you're Clementine's niece, why haven't we ever seen you around here?"

"It's been years since I've seen her. My parents died and I lost all my family connections years ago, living in foster care. A private detective tracked me down."

He considered this and took a walk around the kitchen, looking things over. His eyes were dark and intense. "You'll be selling the place, then? Why didn't you just hire a real estate agent?"

"No, I'm not selling," Erin said firmly. "I'm reopening."

The eyebrows went up again. "This place has been sitting empty for ten years or more. You're reopening Clementine's Tea Room?"

"No, I'll be opening a specialty bakery, once I get everything whipped into shape." She folded her arms across her chest, looking at him challengingly. "I assume you don't have a problem with that?"

"No, ma'am."

But he didn't give any indication of leaving. Erin swept back a few tendrils of dark hair that had slipped from her braid, aware that she was probably looking travel-worn after several days in the car. She had put on mascara and dusty rose lipstick before getting on her way that morning, but she felt gritty and sweaty from travel and would have preferred a shower before having met anyone in her new hometown.

Erin strode toward the front of the store and the policeman moved out of the doorway and then back around the counter toward the front door.

"You shouldn't leave the door wide open."

"I wanted some air in here. I've only been here five minutes. Do the police always show up that fast in Bald Eagle Falls?"

"I just happened by. Thought it was strange to see Clementine's door hanging open. Didn't recognize the car."

"Well, thank you for looking into it." Erin waited until he stepped out onto the sidewalk and then followed, pulling the door shut behind her. He watched as she locked it again. "You see? I have the keys."

"Where did this detective find you?"

"Maine."

"Is that where you're from?"

"I'm from a lot of places. Now I'm looking at settling back down here."

Erin looked at the German Shepherd, doing the doggie equivalent of standing at attention.

"I've never heard of a small town like this having a K9 unit."

"Well," he looked down at the dog, chewing on his words, "this is the extent of our K9 contingent."

"He looks... very well-trained. What's his name?"

"K9."

Erin cracked a smile. "Seriously?"

He kept a serious face, nodding once.

"Okay. Well, again, thank you for checking in on my store, Officer...?"

"Terry Piper."

"Erin Price." Erin offered her hand and this time Piper took it, giving her hand a brief squeeze as if he were afraid of crushing it.

"Pleased to meet you, Miss Price. Or is it missus?"

"It's Miss."

"Keep safe. Give us a call if you need anything." He produced a business card with a blue and yellow crest on it. "We don't exactly have 9-1-1 service but there's always someone on call."

Erin nodded her thanks. "I'll keep it handy. A lot of crime in Bald Eagle Falls?"

"No. It's a sleepy little town. Not too much excitement. Rowdy teenagers. Some of the drug trade trickling down from the city. The occasional domestic."

"Not a lot of break-and-enters?" she teased.

He didn't look amused. "You can't be too careful. Where are you headed now? There's a motel down the way..."

"No. I got the house too. I'll be staying there."

"You can't sleep there tonight. Won't be any water or power."

"They've been turned on. Thanks for your concern."

He looked for something else to say, then apparently couldn't find anything, so he nodded and walked down the sidewalk with his faithful companion.

Erin kept one eye on the GPS and the other on her rearview mirror to see if Officer Piper had any ideas about hopping into his car and following her home to make sure that she was properly situated. But apparently, he couldn't think of any laws she had broken and he never appeared behind her. Clementine's house was only a few blocks away. Erin parked on the street in front of it and took it in. It was a pretty little house with white siding and green shutters, roof peaks, and accents. The living room had big windows to let in the light and a window up at the top peak hinted at an attic bedroom or study. Beside and behind the house, beyond the fence line, were shimmering green, dense woods.

Erin got out of the car and grabbed her suitcase before walking up to the heavy paneled door and inserting her key in the lock. This one didn't stick, but turned smoothly like it was welcoming her home. Erin lugged her suitcase into the front entryway and closed and locked the door behind her. No point in inviting more visitors. She really didn't want to have to deal with anyone else until morning.

The AC was on, so the house wasn't stifling like the shop had been. Erin hadn't been sure what to expect. Burgener, the lawyer, had informed her that the house was furnished, but she hadn't known what kind of state it would be in. But it was neat and tidy. Furnished, but not cluttered. There were a couple of magazines on the coffee table in the living room that were months old, but other than that, Clementine might have just left it a few days before. Or still be in the other room just awaiting Erin's arrival.

She wasn't a believer in ghosts or restless spirits, but Clementine's smell and flavor still clung to the place.

Erin left her suitcase at the door and explored the house slowly. Living room, small dining room, kitchen, Clementine's bedroom, a guest room, and what Erin thought she might call a sewing room. There was fabric, rolls of wrapping paper, partially finished crafts, and post-bound books of genealogy, painstakingly written in longhand.

There were pull-down steps to the attic. If there had only been a ladder, Erin probably wouldn't have explored any further, but the stairs were well-made and modern and raised her hopes that the attic had been properly developed and wasn't just a storage space full of boxes, bags, cobwebs, and dust.

She mounted the stairs. At the top, there was enough light from below to find a light switch. Erin switched it on and had a look around.

It was a beautiful, bright room. Erin knew she was going to be spending a lot of her free time up there. White paneling and built-in cabinetry, soft, natural-looking lighting; it consisted of a reading nook, a writing desk, a comfy-looking couch, and various other touches that would make it a paradisiacal oasis at the end of a tiring day of baking.

Or driving.

After exploring the attic, Erin shut off the light, descended, and pushed the stairs up until the counterbalance took over and raised them to snick softly into place in the ceiling.

Erin returned to the kitchen for a glass of water, not looking forward to the fact that she was going to have to go out and pick up groceries if she wanted anything to eat. She found a sticky note on the fridge on notepaper preprinted with the lawyer's logo and phone number.

Welcome home. You'll find some basic supplies in the fridge. JRB

Erin opened the fridge door and sighed. Milk, juice, eggs, bagels, jam, and some precut fruit and vegetable packs. That and the coffee maker on the counter would do just fine. If James Burgener had been there, she would have hugged him.

A quick snack and then she would be off to the guest room for some shut-eye. Ghosts or not, she wasn't going to be sleeping in the master bedroom until she had made it her own.

Never one to let moss grow, Erin set to work immediately the next morning. She found a sort of a general store which carried both the small appliances she needed and painting supplies. With the back seats folded down, she filled the cargo area of the Challenger with as much as it would hold. She went back to the shop, opened the windows, and prepped the walls to start painting. Best to get a fresh coat of paint on before installing anything new.

"Knock, knock?"

Erin was startled out of her thoughts. She yanked the earbuds out of her ears and turned to face the woman who was trying to get her attention.

"I'm sorry," the woman said, giving her a tentative smile. She had a pleasant face; a middle-aged woman with ash blond hair. Either she had the perfect figure, or her clothes were hand-tailored. "I didn't want to startle you, but you were pretty engrossed…"

Erin wiped her forehead with the back of her hand. "Yeah. A little caught up in my music and my work."

"My name is Mary Lou Cox. I heard a rumor that you were here. So, I just had to come over and extend a good old Bald Eagle Falls welcome."

"Erin Price. I, uh… Clementine was my aunt."

"Well, if you're kin to Clementine, you're kin to half the mountain. Welcome home."

Erin nodded awkwardly. "Thank you. That's very kind of you."

"So…" Mary Lou took a look around the kitchen. "A fresh coat of paint and then I hear you're opening up Clementine's Tea Room again? I'll tell you, this town has surely missed the tea room."

"Uh. No. I'm not reopening the tea room." Erin enjoyed a cup of tea at the end of the day as much as anyone, but she was much more interested in baking. The groove she got into while painting was nothing compared with the nirvana she would achieve while baking. "I'm opening a specialty bakery."

Mary Lou patted her hair. "We already have a bakery in Bald Eagle Falls."

Erin ran the roller down the wall, watching carefully for seams or drips.

"I'm sure the town can support more than one bakery."

"But we already have The Bake Shoppe. We don't need another bakery."

Erin gave her a determined smile. "I'm opening a bakery."

"Angela Plaint owns The Bake Shoppe and does a really nice business, I'm not sure any of us would go to another bakery. It wouldn't be a very loyal thing to do."

"You could go to The Bake Shoppe for… whatever Angela Plaint is best at and then come to my bakery for gluten-free muffins."

"Gluten-free?" Mary Lou echoed.

"I assume you don't already have a gluten-free bakery."

"No, we do not. If you want that kind of baking, you have to drive into the city."

"Well, now you'll be able to get them in town."

"There aren't that many people that want that gluten-free stuff in Bald Eagle Falls. I don't see how you could make a living off it."

"We'll just have to see. I do other specialty baking as well. Dairy-free, allergy-free, vegan."

"We don't have a lot of *those* kind of people here. We like our meat. Whoever put meat in muffins anyway?"

Erin studied Mary Lou for a moment, trying to divine whether she was teasing or being sarcastic. "You might not put meat in a muffin, but you would probably put eggs and dairy."

"And you could make it without all those things? Who would eat such a thing? It would be like eating cardboard."

"Not when I make it."

"I guess we'll just have to see," Mary Lou said. "I sure don't cotton to the idea of you trying to take Angela's business."

"I guess we'll just have to see," Erin echoed.

Mary Lou was the first citizen of Bald Eagle Falls to express her opinion and welcome Erin to town, but she wasn't the last. Next came Melissa Lee, a woman with curly dark hair and a wide, even smile. And then Gema Reed, with her long, steel gray locks and a girlish complexion.

Erin did her best to explain to them that she wasn't there to horn in on Angela's business and take money out of her pocket, but to offer a new service that hadn't previously been available. But it was like talking to the wall. Or yelling at an avalanche. It didn't stop them from dumping advice all over her, while smiling and telling her she was welcome in town.

She didn't feel welcome.

At least Terry Piper did not show up with his K9 to give his input on the matter.

It was a long day and Erin never did meet Angela, her competition. The end of the day, the walls were freshly painted. Everything looked fresh and new. Exhausted though she was, Erin spent a few more minutes in the tiny office, going through the papers and plans in the folders she had brought with her from Maine.

Then she locked everything up tight and headed back home.

Chapter Two

THE DAY DAWNED BRIGHT and clear. Erin woke up earlier than she expected after her hard work of the day before. She was looking forward to each new day, rather than dreading another day of work.

Starting the day in her attic study, Erin wrote up lists of things she would need to get in the city. Not only did Bald Eagle Falls not have a specialty bakery, the general store did not carry any of the specialized flours or other ingredients that she would need. Erin had no intention of taking months getting outfitted. The store and the appliances were on hand and ready for use, so why wait?

It was late when Erin returned to the shop at the end of the day. Darkness was settling over Main Street and the streetlights were few and far between. As she juggled her first armload of goods while trying to unlock the front door, chiding herself for using the front door instead of the back— even though she would have had the same problem at the back—a voice spoke in her ear.

"Can I help you with those?"

The bag of flour she was pressing against the door with her body in an effort to hang on to it while unlocking the bolt was removed from its position. Erin laughed a little and unlocked the door, turning to get the bag of flour back from him.

She froze, looking into the dirty, sweaty face of a man she had never met before. He was white, though the word white did nothing to convey the color of his skin, dirt ground into it as if he had been working in a coal mine or living on the street for weeks. He had a fringe of a mustache and a few bristles on his chin, looking more like he was careless with his shaving than that he had intentionally trimmed his facial hair in a particular style. He had a filthy, army-green cap pulled down low so she could just make out his dark eyes.

"I can take this in for you," he offered. His voice was gravelly and low, but polite. He didn't have the drawl that would indicate he was native to the area.

"Oh, no, let me take it back," Erin said, encircling the bag with her arm and taking its weight.

He looked at her with a sullen expression that told Erin he understood that she didn't want him in her store. She turned her back on him to take the supplies into the kitchen, mentally sorting out possible weapons and escape routes. She was sure he was going to follow her in. Would a scream bring Officer Terry Piper or whoever else might be on shift?

When she went back out to her car for the next load, the man was still hanging around, as she had expected. He took bags out of her car and handed them to her.

"Really," Erin told him politely, "I'm okay. I don't need any help."

He didn't react with anger or violence, but his dark eyes glittered under the bill of his cap. "Just trying to be neighborly."

"I appreciate it. You're very kind. But you're making me nervous."

She surprised herself by telling him that. Was she acting like a victim? Encouraging him to menace her further? She knew from self-defense classes that predators looked for shyness and low self-esteem. Did she sound weak saying he was making her nervous?

But the man immediately backed off, shaking his head. "Not trying to make anyone nervous, miss."

"Then please leave me alone."

He stood there looking at her for a minute, then turned without a word and walked away. Erin blew out her breath, relieved. Here she had thought that moving to a small town in the South, she would be safe from crime and unwanted attention, but obviously nowhere was completely safe. She needed to be realistic instead of idealizing small-town living as being something it wasn't. Next time, she would not be unloading her car after dark. She would plan ahead and be better prepared.

Erin took the rest of the supplies into the kitchen and put them away. She stopped in the office to pick up one of her folders, frowning. She had a strange feeling of vertigo, like everything was slightly out of place. She couldn't identify any one thing that would make her feel that way, but couldn't help feeling like her things had been touched and moved around. She found the folder she was looking for on signage and took it home with her, locking up carefully.

Traffic was even quieter than usual in the sleepy town when Erin got to the shop to finish organizing her ingredients and to make plans for what she would make to kick off her opening and really wow her customers.

She was sitting at her desk in the tiny office, scribbling away and flipping back and forth between recipes when she heard the bells over the front door jingle. She didn't want anyone sneaking up on her today.

Erin reluctantly stood up from her work and went out to the front of the shop. It was Gema Reed, the beautiful gray-haired woman.

"I thought I saw your car outside," Gema declared. She couldn't very well have missed it. It wasn't exactly camouflaged. And it was one of the only vehicles parked on sleepy Main Street. "So, I thought I would drop in and make sure everything was okay?"

Erin tilted her head slightly, trying to figure out where Gema was going with the inquiry.

"Umm, yes. Everything is fine. Why wouldn't it be?"

"Well, being as it's the *Sabbath* and you're at work. I was worried maybe you had a water main break or vandals. Maybe even a fire. You never know what's going to happen."

"No, there's nothing wrong. I just wanted to get some work done. There's lots to do before I open."

They stood there looking at each other awkwardly for a few moments. Erin knew she was moving into the Bible belt, but she hadn't expected things to be that different from the way they had been in the North. Some people were religious and some people were not and everybody observed their beliefs as they wished. But apparently, things were not quite so straightforward in the South.

"Well, maybe no one invited you to Sunday morning services. You probably don't even know the schedule!" Gema proclaimed. "Now there are lots of churches to choose from, of course, but if you want to join us at First Baptist, just down at the end of Main Street and Garity, why, we'd *love* to have you!"

"I'm going to have to pass…" Erin said slowly, feeling her way through. "I'm not really the churchgoing type."

"Not the type? Why, bless your heart, dear, you don't have to be a type to join your fellow Christians at worship on Sunday! You… *are* a Christian, aren't you? Not one of these… other sects? I don't mean to put down Jews or Muslims or anyone else, but here in Bald Eagle Falls, we're Christian. Baptists, Catholics, Protestants, it doesn't matter, as long as you're Christian!"

Erin cleared her throat. She wished she had brought a cloth with her out to the front, so she could occupy herself with polishing the glass and chrome display case and counter. Just to have something to do with her hands and somewhere to look other than Gema Reed's benevolent Christian face. "Actually, Mrs. Reed. I'm not."

"You're not… what? You don't look like a Jew or one of those… pagan people. Not everyone goes to church every Sunday, but…"

"I'm… not Christian. I'm atheist."

"Atheist!" Gema was aghast. She held her hand dramatically at her throat, halfway to covering her mouth in horror. She stared at Erin pleadingly, as if she thought it might just be a clumsy joke and Erin would change her tune. "You're not! Really?"

"Yes. I am. I'm sorry if that upsets you…"

"Well, Jesus loves every humble seeker of the truth. You are a seeker, aren't you? Not everyone can be converted, but as long as you're looking for the truth, you will find it in the end…"

Erin took a deep breath and let it back out again. As much as she wanted to smooth Gema's ruffled feathers, to just reassure her and send her on her way, she wanted to get it out in the open. Her real beliefs, not just rumors or half-baked explanations.

"Mrs. Reed—"

"Gema, sugar…"

"Gema. I am an atheist. Not an agnostic. Not an investigator or a seeker. An atheist. I'm not looking for something to believe in. I already have a belief system. And it doesn't include God."

Gema gasped audibly and this time she did cover up her mouth. "Oh, my dear…"

Erin forced a smile. "I'm not a witch or a devil-worshiper. And I won't try to talk you out of your beliefs. But I, myself, do not believe in God. Not a god of any sort. Not the universe, or Mother Nature, or a higher power, or Jesus. I'm sorry."

"Well." Gema looked for a moment as if she would flee without another word. Instead, she smoothed her waves of silver, took a calming breath and gave a polite nod. "Everybody is entitled to their own opinion, no matter how wrong. I'd better get on my way, or I'll be walking into service late. I just hope… that you won't be encouraging others to break the Sabbath by your blatant disregard for it. You won't have your bakery open on Sunday, will you?"

Erin gave a little shrug. "Didn't my Aunt Clementine have it open after services on Sunday?" she asked tentatively. Her memories of Clementine's Tea Room were startlingly clear in some respects and shrouded by fog in others. She was sure she remembered helping to serve the church ladies after Sunday services. They had all thought her such a cute, pretty young thing. She remembered her resentment over being treated like a puppy or a baby instead of a person with a mind of her own. She loved helping Clementine in the tea room, but she didn't like that part of it.

Gema made a noise of indecision, not wanting to admit that Erin was right and yet compelled by her Christian morals not to tell a lie. "Mmmmm… yes, it is true that she opened up for an hour or two after services on Sunday, so the ladies would have somewhere to go to discuss Christian services required in the upcoming week…"

"So, it would be okay, as long as I waited until after your worship services?"

"As an atheist, I'm not sure it would be the same…"

"I would be shunned for opening my restaurant, but a Christian would not? When it's against a Christian's beliefs, but not mine? Wouldn't it be worse for a Christian to do it?"

"I just don't know," Gema snapped, shaking her head in confusion. "I must get on now, but I'll… I'll think it over."

"Okay…" Erin gave her a little wave. "You be sure to let me know what you ladies decide. Someone mentioned that Clementine's Tea Room had been sorely missed and I thought that if I could provide a similar service…"

Gema Reed gulped. She shook her head and retreated. The bells tinkled behind her and Erin stood there, watching her get into her big red truck and pull out into the street. Then she was gone.

Erin went back to her office to continue working on her opening and marketing strategy. She added 'Sunday social tea' to her list with a wry smile and continued to look through her recipes.

After Erin finished her plans, she carefully filed her folders in the cabinet beside the desk. There was no reason to leave her lists scattered all over her desk and take the chance of losing something when she had a perfectly functional file drawer to put everything neatly away. She emptied the dregs of her cold coffee from her mug and washed it out, leaving it upside down on a towel to dry.

When she stepped out of the shop onto the sidewalk, she nearly collided with a woman coming the other direction. Sunday had been so quiet, she hadn't expected any foot traffic and hadn't even looked before stepping out the door.

"Oh, I'm sorry!" she apologized.

The other woman was ruddy, a redhead, on the plumpish side. Her hair fell in waves around her head, partially obscuring her face. She stepped back from Erin, folding her arms across her chest and staring at Erin as if she had just committed a mortal sin. Which, given Gema's reaction to Erin working on a Sunday, was probably the case.

"I didn't see you coming," Erin apologized. "That was my fault. I'm sorry."

The woman ignored the apology. "You're Clementine's niece."

"Yes, I am."

"You don't favor her, do you?"

"I don't remember her too clearly," Erin admitted. "And I don't really know what she looked like in later years."

"If you don't remember her, then what are you doing here? Why come to Bald Eagle Falls?"

Erin's mouth was dry. She tried to put together words that made sense, flummoxed by the woman's attack.

"I inherited the store and the house. I wanted to reopen the shop."

"Only you're not," the redhead hissed. "You're not reopening the tea room, you're opening a bakery."

"Well, yes. That's what I do, I bake. I'm still planning on serving tea after Sunday services each week, so the women can get together…"

"We don't need another bakery."

Erin sighed and shook her head. "It's a specialty bakery. It means people won't have to go into the city to get gluten-free or allergy-friendly baking. It doesn't directly compete with the other bakery."

"You *are* competing, little Miss Out-of-Towner. And you're not going to last a week!"

With that, the redhead marched on, shouldering past Erin with a force that staggered her and made her catch herself on the side of the building.

Looking across Main Street, she saw Officer Terry Piper watching her, K9 at his side. She considered calling him over to vent about the rude woman, but decided that would just be sour grapes. She didn't really want to charge the woman. There was no point in reporting the encounter to the police.

Erin yawned as she pushed open her door, sending the little bells tinkling in welcome. She was going to have to get used to getting up early if she were going to be running a bakery. She was going to have to get up while it was still dark and everyone else was sleeping in order to have freshly baked goods in the display cases when people started walking in for a little something to go with their coffees or office meetings.

Her day would start way before anyone else's and, if she were going to stay open past afternoon, she was going to need to find an assistant to split shifts with. It wouldn't have to be another baker, just someone who could answer questions about ingredients and work the cash register.

Taking into account the not-so-warm reaction she was getting from the women of the town, she might have to go to the city to find someone willing to work the bakery.

Erin juggled her keys and her bag of groceries to turn on the kitchen light and put her bag on the counter.

Her coffee mug lay on the floor, shattered. Erin frowned and looked around. A shiver ran down her spine. Had someone been there? Had her shop been broken into?

For a few moments, she just stood there, frozen, listening for any movement.

There was only silence. She considered the situation. Had she put the mug too close to the edge of the counter and it had fallen off by itself? Were there earthquakes in Tennessee?

The imprint of the mug was still in the towel she had left it sitting on. Close to the edge of the counter, but not over it.

She heard the bells on the front door ring and hurried out to see whether someone was leaving the shop. Had she actually walked right past an intruder? Maybe hiding behind the counter, below her eye level while she yawned and juggled her groceries in the morning dimness?

She stopped stock-still. Nobody had left the shop; wild-haired Melissa Lee had come in. She was all smiles and sweetness, launching into a long-winded description of some fundraiser that she and some of the other women were running. She cut herself off abruptly.

"My dear, you look like you've just seen a ghost. Are you okay?"

"I… I think someone has been in here."

"What do you mean, in here?" she asked doubtfully.

"I think someone broke in…"

"You have been burgled?" Melissa's voice rose, a mixture of disbelief and alarm. Such things were probably unheard of in sleepy little Bald Eagle Falls. "Honey, you stay right there while I get the police."

Melissa hurried back out the front door and, without a clue what else to do, Erin obeyed, standing there like a statue.

It was only a few minutes before Melissa returned, Officer Terry Piper in tow with his K9. Melissa was babbling on about crime rates and burglaries. Piper ignored her and focused on Erin.

"The place was broken into?" he demanded.

"I don't know. I think someone has been here."

Feeling embarrassed that she might be overreacting, Erin took him into the kitchen and showed him the broken mug and where it had been sitting on the counter. Piper nodded and looked around, his brows drawn down.

"Anyone else have a key?" he asked.

K9 sniffed at the broken mug with interest, but didn't lead his master along a scent trail. He just sat back on his haunches and panted.

"No. I haven't given anyone else a key."

Piper looked into the small office. "Anything been touched in here? Anything missing?"

Erin hadn't yet had a chance to look. She gave a little laugh and slipped by him to see. The room looked untouched. Erin checked her file drawers.

"There was one other time… when I thought things had been moved in here. I put everything away in my drawers, this time…"

"Do you have petty cash in here? A safe?"

"No. Nothing like that. And no cash in the register yet, either. I haven't opened for business yet." She knew she didn't really need to add that part. Terry Piper was undoubtedly aware that she hadn't yet opened to the public. If there had been any doubt, the fact that there were no baked goods in the display case or in the oven would pretty much be a giveaway.

"When are you opening?" he asked. "Assuming you still are?"

"Yes, of course. I'm just putting together my plans for a small opening celebration right now. A few days…"

He raised an eyebrow. "That quickly? I thought it would take longer to get things up and running."

"Everything is already in place. I've bought supplies. I am still waiting on signage and a few little things like that, but for the time being, I'll just put a handmade sign in the window."

He pursed his lips and nodded. He and K9 went to the back door and examined it to confirm it was still locked and had not been tampered with. He looked at the steep stairs to the basement.

"What have you got downstairs?"

"Storage and the commode. I haven't been down there yet this morning…"

K9's ears pointed down the stairs curiously.

"Does he hear something?" Erin asked.

"No… not yet. Come on, K9. Let's go investigate."

The dog eagerly led the way down the stairs. Erin realized she was holding herself tense and she tried to relax. There wasn't anything downstairs. She already knew it. There had been no sign of forced entry at either door. No open windows somebody might have crawled in through. She was going to have to accept that there had been a tremor or something else that had made the counter shake and caused her coffee mug to go crashing to the floor. The shops were all connected; perhaps someone had dropped a pallet of books with enough force in the bookstore next door that it had shaken the shared wall and sent her mug on its kamikaze journey.

There were no sounds of conflict downstairs. No sign that the officer had found anyone lurking below them. He was back up the stairs in a minute.

"All clear."

They went back out to the front, where Melissa was anxiously waiting. Piper examined the front door and frame.

"There aren't any signs of forced entry," he said with a shrug. "Is it possible you left it unlocked last night?"

"No, I'm sure I…" Erin remembered colliding with the woman on the sidewalk as she left. Had she locked the door afterward? Erin knew she had unlocked the door in the morning. And it could only be locked from the outside. If she'd had to unlock it in the morning, then she had locked it the night before. "Yes. I'm sure I locked it. It was locked when I came in this morning."

"Maybe you knocked the mug down without realizing it, last night or this morning. Or maybe a crosswind or the building shaking for some reason?" Piper shrugged.

"It's a mystery!" Melissa said in dramatic tones.

Piper gave her a tolerant smile. "Yes, Mrs. Lee. It surely is."

"Maybe it's a ghost! The tea shop is haunted."

"Bakery," Erin corrected, aware she was nitpicking, but irritated about the community's opposition to a second bakery opening.

"We haven't had a ghost here before," Melissa enthused. "I wonder who it could be. There are a lot of civil war ghosts in the area. We have a rich civil war history, you know. Why, the library is practically famous in these parts. There are so many legends of lost and buried treasure in the hills around here, a person can hardly go for a hike without tripping over one!" She laughed.

"If there hasn't been a ghost here before," Piper said gravely, "then the ghost must be of a more recent vintage, wouldn't you say?"

Melissa stopped and considered. "Well, yes, I suppose. Unless you've somehow awoken a restless spirit. You haven't been digging down there in your basement? Or in the back?"

"No," Erin assured her. "The basement floor is concrete and so is the parking lot in back."

"Then we need to think of who might have died recently that would have a reason to haunt the store." Melissa pondered the problem.

Erin exchanged looks with Piper. He appeared to be suppressing a smile.

"Maybe… the owner?" he suggested.

"Erin?" Melissa said blankly.

"The… previous owner…?" Piper prompted.

"Oh, Clementine! Why, of course it would be Clementine! Silly old me!" She put her hand on Erin's arm. Her dark curls quivered with her movement. "You are being haunted by your Aunt Clementine. Did you have any unfinished business with her? Something that she would be expecting from you?"

"Just opening the bakery. And why, if there was such a thing as ghosts, would my aunt's restless spirit want to break my coffee mug?"

"She's trying to reach you, dear. Ghosts are very limited in what they can do. Move things, appear to you, maybe make noises. It's not like on TV, where they can just walk up and talk to you and explain themselves in words. All she can do to reach you is to move things around."

Erin nodded. "I see. Well, I don't believe in ghosts, so I'm going to look for more earthly explanations. You can… believe what you like."

"Oh, I do," Melissa agreed. "I am going to talk to the others and we'll see if we can sort this out. After all, we all knew Clementine. I knew her my whole life. We'll figure out what it is that she wants to reach you for. Mary Lou's sister-in-law, she's very good with spirits. We'll see if she can come here and make contact with your poor dead auntie."

Erin glanced over at Piper, widening her eyes, sure she was being played. But Piper gave no sign that Melissa was joking. And Melissa continued to look earnest and excited about the whole ghost business.

"Isn't contacting ghosts considered sorcery in Christian circles?" Erin suggested.

"No, no! Mary Lou's sister-in-law won't be using a Ouija board or any other devil's tool. She just uses prayer. There's nothing wrong with that."

"Ah." Erin nodded. She looked at her watch as obviously as possible. Time was trickling by and she had work to do. "Did you want to leave me a flyer about your fundraiser,

Melissa?" At Melissa's blank look, she indicated the woman's clipboard. "That was why you came in here, wasn't it?"

"Oh, yes!" Melissa pulled a fuchsia-colored page from her clipboard and handed it to Erin. "Of course, no one is required to donate or put time into it, but every little bit is appreciated! I'd better get on my way! If I stop to yap at every store, it's going to take me all day! I'm already busier than a one-armed paper hanger."

Erin nodded and gave a little wave, and Melissa went on her way. Erin sighed and looked at Officer Piper. He had a gorgeous smile, when he let it show.

"Miss Price, I'm sorry I couldn't be of more assistance. You feel free to call on me if you have any more troubles. Hopefully, your ghost won't cause any more trouble."

"Thanks," Erin said dryly. "Just tell me… everyone in town doesn't believe that, do they? In the existence of ghosts, I mean? And that they can just… be contacted?"

"Not everyone is quite as literal as Mrs. Lee, but… I do imagine most of them will agree that your shop might be haunted. They might not be willing to say that it is, but they won't say that it isn't…"

Erin shook her head. "I suppose it's harmless, as long as they aren't demanding to hold 17éances in here."

Chapter Three

ERIN HAD DONE EVERYTHING she could to prepare for opening. She had taken out an ad in the Pennysaver, had delivered flyers to all the surrounding businesses, had put her handlettered 'Auntie Clem's Bakery' sign up in the window. She was up at three in the morning to start baking. Some of her batters and breads had been prepared and chilled or frozen ahead of time, but it still took time to bake a wide enough variety of treats to interest a new clientele.

The kitchen smells were heavenly and she was looking forward to propping open the front door to get some cross-ventilation, which would also help to spread the delicious scents and bring in walk-by traffic.

Wiping her forehead with the back of her forearm, Erin paused for a moment before taking out a batch of blueberry muffins. Her stomach was growling and it was time to sample some of her own goods. Blueberries were always a favorite of hers. Even better than chocolate chips.

After putting a variety of goods in the display case, Erin went to the front door. She was ten minutes early, but there were people hovering around the door. She took a calming breath and arranged a smile on her face. Then she opened the door.

She had been afraid that no one would come after all the remonstrations that the town didn't need another bakery. How many people with special diets were there in the population? Would people who didn't have any special needs still come by to check it out? But there were a couple of businessmen with tall cups of coffee, and a mother with four children of varying sizes, both sophisticated Mary Lou and sturdy, gray-haired Gema Reed, and a few faces Erin didn't know. She let the fresh air breeze in, displacing the warm, fragrant air.

"Ooooh," the children sighed as they smelled all the baked goods.

One little boy of six or seven tugged on Erin's apron. "We get a free cookie?"

"Yes! A free cookie or a muffin. A special opening-day treat!"

He darted over to the display case and pressed his hands and face against the glass, peering in at the cookies.

"Which ones don't have wheat?" he demanded. "My tummy can't have wheat."

"None of them have wheat," Erin told him.

The boy's mouth dropped open. "Are you *sure*?"

"I'm sure. I made them myself."

He studied her seriously, his brows drawing down. "Do they have white flour? White flour is still wheat."

"No, they have superfine rice flour and cornstarch. Or other flours. And some of them have oats. I know oats still bother some people, so those ones are all marked."

"Certified gluten-free oats? Or oats from the grocery store?" he interrogated.

"Certified gluten-free."

The boy looked at his mother. Erin looked at her as well. "He knows his stuff, doesn't he?"

"We've had plenty of experience. He's learned how to advocate for himself." She beamed with pride, jiggling a pink-cheeked baby tied to her in a sling.

The boy went back to peering at the cookies, considering his options. He had probably never had a choice of bakery-fresh cookies before.

Erin went back behind the counter and started to serve up the complimentary cookies and muffins. The mother of the little boy bought a couple of loaves of bread and some muffins for breakfast the next day. The little boy, whose name was Peter Foster, settled on a chocolate chip oatmeal cookie, the chips still warm and gooey. At Peter's suggestion, his sisters chose a gingersnap and a macaroon, so that each could have a taste of three different kinds of cookies and decide which kind they liked best.

Erin was waving goodbye to Peter and his family when the angry redhead came in through the door. Erin froze there with her hand up like an idiot, wondering what the woman was doing coming into the store. The other ladies greeted her, but she didn't smile and make nice. She seemed to have a permanent scowl. She made her way to the display case and looked down at the baked goods.

"Everything here is gluten-free?"

"Yes. It's all gluten-free."

"So, you don't even have any wheat or other gluten flour in the kitchen?"

"No. Completely clean. All gluten-free."

She scowled down at the cookies.

"There is a free cookie or muffin for every customer today," Erin offered, forcing a smile. It felt plastic and unnatural. Like it belonged on someone else's face.

"I am highly allergic to wheat. If you use any in the kitchen, I will know it."

"I don't. And none of the pans or implements have been used for anything but gluten-free cooking. There is no chance of cross-contamination."

The other ladies were watching the redhead, no longer pretending to have their own conversations. It was just Mary Lou, Melissa, and Gema. Everyone else had eaten their free treat, placed their orders, and gone.

.

The redhead turned around and looked at the women, giving them a glare that made them huddle around their treats and giggle nervously, hiding their mouths behind their hands.

"I'll have a chocolate muffin," the woman announced, turning back to Erin so suddenly that she just about dropped her tongs.

"Oh. Okay," Erin agreed. She selected one of the chocolate muffins and passed it across the counter. "My name is Erin Price."

"I know who you are." The redhead took a bite of the chocolate muffin and chewed slowly. "Not bad," she admitted. "I'm Angela Plaint."

"*You're* Angela Plaint?" Erin was floored. This was the owner of The Bake Shoppe? Highly allergic to wheat and running a traditional bakery? No wonder the woman was bitter.

"Yes."

"Oh…" Erin spluttered, looking for something to say. "Well… I'm glad you came to my opening. Would you like anything to take home?"

"Six of these."

Erin packed up six chocolate muffins and took Angela's money, feeling unaccountably guilty. Why should she feel bad about selling to the competition? It wasn't like Angela was going to resell them in her own bakery for a profit. She just wanted something for later. If she were the only one in her family who was allergic, she would probably freeze the muffins individually to keep them fresh, thawing out one at a time as she needed them.

Erin couldn't think of anything else to say to Angela. She realized belatedly that Angela was talking to her. Asking a question.

"I'm sorry, what?"

"Is this the commode?" Angela pointed to the door to the stairs. She could see the ladies'/men's placard, so Erin wasn't sure why she was asking.

"Yes. Down the stairs. I'm sorry about that, it's not very accessible."

"No," Angela sneered. "It's not."

She opened the door and headed down the stairs. There was no one else at the counter, so Erin went over to talk to Mary Lou, Melissa, and Gema.

"That's my competition?" she asked in a whisper. "Why didn't anyone tell me she was allergic to wheat? Doesn't she sell any gluten-free products?"

"No, no," Melissa shook her head, eyes wide, curls bouncing wildly. "She doesn't do the baking anymore, because the flour in the air would make her sick. She just owns the place. And if they made gluten-free goods, they would be contaminated with the flour in the air and on the same equipment. She wouldn't be able to eat them."

"I guess not," Erin admitted. "Why on earth does she own a bakery?"

"She used to be a wonderful baker," Gema said, eyes distant. "She loved to bake and she was at it sun-up to sundown. And then one day... she just started to get sick. She couldn't eat wheat, or breathe it, or touch it. There was no way she could keep it up. She had to hire bakers and can't even go into the bakery while they are cooking. If no one is baking, she can go in for a few minutes, as long as she doesn't touch anything."

"I can't imagine. Why didn't she just sell the business and start something else?"

Mary Lou smoothed her pastel pant suit and gave a wide shrug. "Angela Plaint is as stubborn as a mule. She doesn't want to give up what she loves, even if she can't literally have her hands in the business anymore. Nothing is going to keep her from the baking business."

Erin shook her head slowly. She looked toward the door to the stairs and retreated to the serving counter, not wanting Angela to find Erin gossiping about her when she returned.

An older couple came in the front door, moving slowly, the husband with a walker and the wife with a cane. Both had to talk over all the options in the display case, going over them several times, asking Erin for her advice, and bouncing ideas back and forth.

"Where is your rice flour from?" wondered the elderly woman, who had introduced herself as Betty. "Is it from California rice or Chinese rice?"

Erin blinked. "I honestly have no idea."

"Maybe you could go and look? See what is says on the package? I worry about all the arsenic, you know."

"Uh, right," Erin agreed. "If you can wait just a minute… I'll go check."

She took a glance toward the door to make sure no one else was getting impatient with the elderly couple dithering about and then ducked into the kitchen. She scrutinized the various labels on the rice flour, then returned to the front of the store.

"It looks like it's domestic," she said. "Not from China."

"Hmm… maybe we should go with something with oats in it, so it's not *all* rice flour," Betty suggested, looking at her husband.

"They are actually all blends of flours," Erin explained. Not just rice, but sorghum, corn, millet, buckwheat… and some of them have oats, like you said…"

More discussion and interrogation ensued, and two more trips to the kitchen to scrutinize labels.

At last, their bag full of gluten-free goods of varying types, they toddled off again. When she looked around the front of the store, she saw that only Mary Lou remained, savoring a blueberry muffin with a takeout cup of tea, looking though her agenda.

"Blueberry is my favorite," Erin told her.

Mary Lou looked up from her agenda, giving Erin a reserved smile. "Mine too. And I would never guess that it was gluten-free. Most of the gluten-free baking that I've tasted is either gritty or like cardboard. Or it's full of kale or some other weird superfood that nobody in their right mind would put in a dessert."

"Blueberries are a superfood. I'd much rather have blueberries in a muffin than kale!"

"Me too!"

Mary Lou looked down at her agenda for another minute, writing something down. She looked up.

"Do you think you should check on Angela? She's been an awfully long time."

Erin's stomach clenched. She looked toward the stairs. "Didn't she come back up? I just assumed I missed her leaving while that lovely couple was here…"

"No. Not unless she went the back way."

"I have the other door locked. Can't have customers marching through the kitchen."

Mary Lou looked at the closed stairway door. Erin went around the counter and opened it. She peeked down the stairs, afraid she was going to find Angela sprawled there with a head injury or a broken leg. How would a major insurance claim on her first day of business go over? And what would that do to her sales?

"Uh… Angela? Are you okay?" she called down.

There was no response. But if Angela was in the bathroom with the door shut, or had just flushed the commode or was running water, she wouldn't be able to hear a thing. Erin felt like she was being intrusive going down the stairs to check on Angela, but if Mary Lou was right and Angela had not slipped past without either of them seeing her, something could be really wrong.

"Angela?" Erin started down the stairs.

Behind her, Mary Lou got up from her table and walked to the doorway, looking down.

"Is she there?"

"I don't know yet…"

Erin turned the corner and stopped.

It was worse than she had imagined. Worse than her worst nightmares of all the things that might go wrong on opening day. *What if nobody came? What if someone complained about the baking? What if she didn't sell a thing?*

It was worse than all of that.

Chapter Four

"ARE YOU OKAY, MISS Price?"

Erin took another sip of her water and nodded.

"Do you think you can answer some questions now?"

"I—I don't know. I—it was so awful!"

"I need you to tell me step-by-step what you saw. Everything. Every impression."

Erin took a deep breath. Her head was still whirling. She wasn't sure how she had ended up sitting in the chair Mary Lou had previously occupied, by the front window of the shop. She wasn't sure at all that she'd climbed the stairs of her own accord. Officer Terry Piper, hovering over her now, might have carried her, or helped her get up the stairs again. She wasn't really sure.

"Where's Mary Lou? Is she okay?" Erin asked.

"Mary Lou is just fine. You will be able to talk to her later. For now, we need to keep the two of you apart."

"Why?"

Piper just looked at her and didn't answer her question. "Tell me what happened."

"I just went downstairs. It had been too long. I thought she might have fallen and hit her head. I was worried about insurance."

"Start at the beginning. What made you go downstairs?"

"Mary Lou. She said that Angela hadn't come back up. Angela went down to use the commode… and she never came back up again."

"What did Mary Lou have to do with it?"

"Nothing. She was just there. She just noticed that Angela hadn't come back out. We decided I should go down and see. Make sure she wasn't sick or hurt."

"Why did you think she might be sick or hurt? Why were you worried about your insurance?"

"I didn't have any reason. Just that she hadn't come back up. The most logical reason was that she was sick. Or hurt. She'd had an accident, hit her head, maybe. And so I just needed to go check, make sure."

"It was Mary Lou's suggestion?"

"Yes."

"You never heard Mrs. Plaint call out? There was no noise from downstairs?"

"No. Nothing. I was serving customers up here. There wasn't any noise from downstairs."

"Did you call down to her?"

"Yes."

"Why? Why didn't you just go down?"

"It just seemed… intrusive. I didn't want her to think that I was checking up on her, if she was just stuck in the commode for longer than usual. I didn't want to embarrass her."

"Okay. Go on. So, you called her and then you went down the stairs."

"I called her again, partway down, in case she just didn't hear me the first time. Flushing the toilet or something."

"And still, no answer."

Erin gave him a look. He knew very well that Angela couldn't have answered. "No. No answer. Not a sound."

"And what did you see when you got to the bottom of the stairs?"

"I went around the corner and there she was…"

"Describe what you found." His pen hovered over his notebook, waiting.

"You know what I found, because it's exactly the same thing as you found when you went down there."

"Please tell me what you saw."

"I saw Angela Plaint. On the floor. Dead."

Chapter Five

W HAT DO YOU THINK Mrs. Plaint died of?" Piper asked.

Erin took another sip of her water. It all seemed so strange. She felt removed from the situation. Like Piper was questioning someone else. Time was elastic, stretching out forever, and then snapping back into place, propelling her forward much too fast. She rubbed her temples.

"I guess… she choked or had an allergic reaction?"

"Why do you think that?"

"Her face was all… purple. And swollen. And her skin… she had welts. Wheals. Hives. She must have eaten something she was allergic to. She wouldn't get hives from choking."

"Uh-huh…"

"But the only thing she ate was one of the chocolate muffins. And they don't have any wheat in them. She told me she was deathly allergic to wheat, but there is no wheat in the place. None at all."

"She didn't tell you if she had any other allergies?"

"No, nothing. Wheat was all that she mentioned."

"And the muffin couldn't have been contaminated from something else? Or she ran across something downstairs that was contaminated?"

"No. Not unless it was contaminated at the factory before I bought it. That's the only possibility I can think of… accidental cross-contamination at the factory. I haven't brought anything with wheat in it into the building."

Piper wrote a few words down. "What was it that made you decide to open a gluten-free bakery? Are you allergic to gluten yourself?"

"No... one of my foster sisters was gluten intolerant... I was really good at cooking up things she could eat. Back then, there wasn't much available commercially. You had to improvise. Experiment with different ingredients. Pick up alternate flours at import stores. It wasn't like it is now, with so much available in grocery stores and health food stores."

"What happened to your foster sister?"

There was an iron knot in Erin's stomach. "What...?"

"You said your foster sister *was* gluten intolerant. That could mean a lot of different things. It could mean that you were only foster sisters for a short period of time and then you were separated and didn't keep in touch. Or..."

Erin seriously considered lying. What were the odds that Piper would actually check her answer? Erin had been through lots of foster sisters in her lifetime. There were plenty of them she no longer kept in touch with. It was such an easy answer. She *was* my sister, she isn't anymore.

"No. She died."

"She died. Was it related to her gluten allergy?"

"Intolerance. Yes, it was."

"How did that happen?"

"She didn't stay compliant. She didn't like having to eat gluten-free all the time and she cheated. She couldn't stick to the diet."

"And that could kill someone who was just gluten-intolerant? She didn't actually have an allergy, so how could it kill her?"

Erin took a deep breath. It was easier to answer an academic question than it was to talk about finding Angela's body, or explaining what had happened to Carolyn.

"A lot of people think that allergy means you have a bad reaction and intolerant means you have a mild reaction. But that's not the difference. An allergy means you have a histamine reaction. An intolerance means that you have another kind of reaction. You can have a mild allergy, maybe a bit of itching or a stomachache, or you can have a severe allergy that causes anaphylaxis and is life-threatening. You can have a minor intolerance, where you can eat a certain amount of a substance without reacting, or where you don't even realize you are having a reaction because there is no pain or discomfort, or you can have an intolerance that is life-threatening."

She stopped and took a sip of water.

"My foster sister kept cheating on her diet and that caused damage to her intestinal tract. They tried to repair it, tried to keep her on a strict gluten-free diet, but she wouldn't comply and nothing they did helped. She lost weight, couldn't absorb nutrients from anything she ate… until she just wasted away."

Erin blinked her eyes rapidly and wiped away tears. "But that was Carolyn. That's not the same as what happened to Angela."

"So, you decided to do something for others who had gluten intolerance. You went into specialty baking."

"Not right away. It was just a hobby. Something I did on the side, for friends who were intolerant or on special diets. Just because it was something I enjoyed doing, and they appreciated it so much, and… it did help me to feel better about Carolyn. Like maybe I could help someone else stay on a gluten-free diet and save their life like no one had been able to do for Carolyn."

"When did it become a business?"

Erin sighed. "Today. Today was the first day that I was a professional gluten-free baker. The first day that it wasn't just a hobby, but my job."

"I see. So you don't have any professional experience."

"No. Plenty of experience, but not professional until today."

"And you haven't run a bakery or eatery before."

"I've worked at restaurants before. I even helped Clementine with the tea room when I was just a little child. I've always been interested in the food industry."

"You've run a restaurant before? Or a bakery?"

"No. Just worked at one."

"And what was your profession in Maine? You were a food service worker?"

"No," Erin admitted reluctantly, "I was a bookkeeper."

"I see." Piper made a few additional notes in his notepad.

Erin shifted uncomfortably in her chair and held her glass against her forehead. "I know what I'm doing," she told him. "Just because I haven't run a bakery before, that doesn't mean that I don't understand the rules and laws involved. And I know more about cross-contamination and how sick gluten or allergies can make someone than anyone. I didn't make a mistake and… kill Angela."

"As far as you know."

Erin looked for a way to argue with the statement. "Well… no," she agreed finally. She obviously couldn't say that she knew more than she knew. "As far as I know."

He turned the page on his notepad. "What was the beef between you and Mrs. Plaint?"

"I… beg your pardon?"

"Easy enough question. The two of you didn't get along. Why not?"

"I didn't even know her."

He stared at her for a few seconds, impassive. That smile that had peeked out when he was discussing ghosts with Melissa Lee was nowhere in evidence. He was on the job. Dead serious.

"I witnessed an altercation between you and Mrs. Plaint myself."

A wave of nausea washed over Erin as the images of her collision with Angela on the sidewalk in front of the store flashed through her mind.

"That wasn't an altercation. I just bumped into her as I left the store. I'd never even met her before that and I didn't know who she was at the time. She didn't tell me her name until today."

"The two of you had a very... intense conversation, for two people who didn't know each other."

"I..." Erin stared out the window at the place where she and Angela had stood on the sidewalk, replaying what she could remember of the conversation. "I didn't know who she was, but she knew who I was. Started up on the same old nonsense about how Bald Eagle Falls already had a bakery and didn't need another one. I didn't even know that she was the owner. She just started in on me, saying that I shouldn't compete with The Bake Shoppe."

He scratched down a few notes. Erin's face was warm.

"The 'same old nonsense,'" Piper repeated slowly, as he wrote the phrase down. "So, you had discussed this with Mrs. Plaint before."

"No! Not with her. Just with the other ladies. Everyone thought I should reopen as Clementine's Tea Room, not as a business in competition with the bakery. When Clementine was running the tea room, she did very little of her own baking. Most of what she sold here, she bought. I don't know if it was from Angela Plaint's bakery, or if that even existed when I was a little girl. Everybody kept saying that I shouldn't compete with Angela."

"And now you won't have to. Now we'll be down to one bakery again."

Erin's stomach twisted and gurgled. "Are you implying that I deliberately killed Angela Plaint with contaminated muffins?" she demanded. "Maybe I should be calling a lawyer."

"No one is making any accusations right now. This is a routine investigation. Of course, you have the right to have your lawyer present during any questioning."

"I don't know what happened to Angela Plaint. But I didn't have anything to do with it. I think we're done here."

"Okay. Thank you for your cooperation." Piper snapped his notepad shut. But he gave no indication he intended to leave.

"I'll call you if I think of anything else," Erin told him, looking significantly toward the door.

"I'll just supervise while you lock up. The business will be off-limits during our investigation. I'll let you know when we release the scene."

"This is my shop!"

"Yes, ma'am. And this is an investigation into a sudden, unexpected death. I will be sealing the doors and you will not be allowed back in until the police department releases it to you. You won't be able to take anything from the scene."

"She died from an allergic reaction! You can't possibly be implying there was foul play involved."

"We will need to make that determination. We don't have Cause of Death yet."

"I have a business to run! How long will this take?"

"I'll let you know when we're finished processing all the evidence."

It took Erin a long time to get to sleep. She felt sick and run down by the end of the day and thought that after getting home, she would just fall into bed and sleep for twelve hours. After all, she had been up since three o'clock, had run her grand opening, and had found a body and dealt with a police investigation. It was enough to wipe anyone out. But when she got home, she didn't climb into bed. She was so angry and worked up, she couldn't even look at her bed.

She rummaged through the fridge for something nourishing to eat. She had planned to bring home a loaf of bread and some muffins from the bakery for her supper and breakfast, but Officer Terry Piper had advised her that she wasn't allowed to take anything home, not even a crumb of bread. It would all have to be tested, he said, to see if any of it was contaminated with wheat or any other substance that might account for Angela's sudden demise. She was left with the fruits and vegetables in the fridge, some cold cereal, and coffee. Whatever was left of the bagels. Not the best dinner.

Of course, she could have gone out to eat. There was a family restaurant in town that boasted 'meat plus three' on the big sign with removable letters outside the building. There was a BBQ place with a special on hot chicken. There was even a little Chinese restaurant that always seemed to have a full parking lot. But Erin wasn't up to appearing in public or dealing with anyone over the phone for takeout. She couldn't stand to think of the management of those places whispering behind her back about her. *Do you know who just ordered the baby back ribs? That woman who murdered Angela Plaint!*

After her unsatisfying meal—what she really wanted was a pint of Ben and Jerry's—she went up to the attic with a cup of coffee. She had a few notes on her plan for the grand opening on her writing desk, though most of her papers were at the office, inaccessible during the police investigation into Angela's death. Even though she had been writing down her lists and plans less than twenty-four hours before, Erin felt like years had passed. Had she really been that excited about opening up? Naive enough to believe everything would go off without a hitch? She had been worried about what she should bake and how she should display it. Worried that no one would show up at the opening. It had never occurred to her that one of her customers would be so inconsiderate as to die on the premises, immediately after eating Erin's baked goods. Erin had been a naive little girl, acting no older than the five-year-old who had helped Auntie Clementine serve the church ladies their tea and cookies.

She tried reading in her little nook, but couldn't focus on the page. Couldn't find anything that interested her. She found herself staring at the wall, going over and over the events of that day and the discussion with Piper. She hadn't made herself look good. Piper thought she was an irresponsible, inexperienced girl pretending she knew what she was doing, a hazard to all her customers.

She paced back and forth across the attic for long hours before she was tired enough to go to bed, almost twenty-four hours after she had gotten up to bake for the opening. And then, even when she lay down, the events of the day kept playing over and over again.

Erin slept fitfully, tossing and turning all night long. Despite the fact that she didn't have to get up to run Auntie Clem's, her brain wouldn't shut off and let her sleep even long after the sun was up.

She dragged herself out of bed and wandered out to the kitchen, looking sadly through the cupboards. She didn't even have any baking supplies at home. Everything was at Auntie Clem's.

The doorbell rang. Erin looked at the cat clock with a swinging tail on the kitchen wall. It was too early for visitors. She felt sick as she considered whether it might be Officer Piper, there to ask her more questions or charge her with something in connection with Angela's death. What would she do? Who would she call? Surely he wouldn't put her in jail. Not over an accident.

With a feeling of dread and her heart pounding, Erin went to the door. It wasn't Officer Piper, but Gema Reed. Erin swung the door open wide.

"Gema?" She stopped herself from asking what she was doing there. Gema held a cardboard tray with two cups of takeout coffee and a brown paper bag.

"I figured you could use some company and a real breakfast this morning," Gema said. "Did I wake you up?"

Erin smoothed her messy bedhead. Gema's gray hair was pulled into a neat ponytail and she looked polished and professional and there Erin was in her ratty housecoat, hair a mess, makeup-less. She guessed by the scratchiness of her eyeballs that they were probably bloodshot.

"You'll feel more human once you've had some java and fuel," Gema assured her. She entered and Erin ushered Gema into the kitchen to sit at the table.

Gema looked around. "You haven't changed anything."

"No. Not yet. I'll add my own touches... sometime."

Gema nodded understandingly. "When you're more comfortable with it being your own."

Erin shrugged. Gema passed her one of the tall coffees and indicated the sugar and creamer packets. "I don't know how you take it." She opened the paper bag and pulled out a couple of chocolate chip muffins that looked suspiciously like Erin's own. "I didn't know what you could eat, so I thought I was best going with something you had made," Gema said with a laugh.

Erin smiled. "I actually don't have any special dietary needs. It's a passion, not a necessity. But I do enjoy the fruits of my labor. Thank you, this was really thoughtful of you. I'm feeling a little... off-kilter this morning. I just don't know what to do with myself."

Gema took a sip of her coffee, her eyes wide. "Wasn't that just the craziest thing you've ever heard? Fancy Angela dying like that, right in your bakery! After all the close calls she has had, she dies in the one place that should have been safe." She covered her mouth. "I don't mean it was your fault, of course, or that your bakery wasn't safe, except... it wasn't!"

"She'd had a lot of close calls?"

"Oh, Dinah! Had she! Why, everyone in town knew about her allergy and about her carrying one of those pen-needles? If she ever had an attack, she said, just pull off the cap and jab it straight into her leg and hold it in there a while. I don't know if I ever could have done it myself. I cringe over popping balloons!"

"I wish someone had been there to do it. When I think about her down in the basement, all alone, with no one to help her..." Erin trailed off. Gema's expression sobered and she looked down.

They both picked at their muffins for a few minutes, thinking over it.

"Such a tragedy," Gema said. "Always sad to see a life cut short."

But Erin thought she seemed just a little too philosophical over it. She had thought that they were friends, that all the women who had visited her and declared their loyalty to the established bakery were friends of Angela's. But Gema wasn't with her church friends, mourning the loss together. She was breaking bread—or muffins—with Erin, the instrument of Angela's death.

"Had you known Angela for long?" Erin asked.

"Well, now, she's not my generation, but I reckon I've known of her since she was born. I can't say we spent a lot of time together, but I knew who she was and I was at the bakery every week. Everyone was."

"Only she hasn't been at the bakery, because of her allergy."

"No, you're right. Not since she developed the allergy. But before that, she was there every week for years. I got accustomed to her."

It was awkward phrasing. They hadn't become friends. Gema had gotten accustomed to Angela.

"You weren't close, then."

"No…" Gema considered her words carefully. "Angela was a hard woman to know. She'd led a hard life. She could come across as… unfriendly. But she was an excellent businesswoman. She had a real knack for it. Not a lot of women do. Not naturally."

"Just the bakery, or other businesses as well?"

Gema scraped her thumbnail along the waxy coating of the coffee cup, looking intent.

"Seems like she always had something on the go. Investments, promotions, new ideas of things that needed to be done around the town or to make a little extra money. She had her finger in a lot of pies."

Erin attempted a joke. "But not literally."

Gema stared at her with wide, surprised eyes and Erin suddenly had a sinking feeling that she had misjudged the situation and it was too soon after Angela's death to joke. She was about to apologize when Gema burst into laughter. Wide, open-mouthed, side-splitting laughter. "Not literally!" she repeated, barely able to catch her breath. "No, definitely not literally!"

Erin was feeling a lot better after Gema's visit. The coffee, baked goods, and companionable conversation had soothed her soul, and she was feeling less out of sorts and more like herself. She had the energy to take a shower and get dressed, deciding she would try reading in the nook in the attic again. Having had a chance to rest and to talk about the accident, maybe she would be less distracted and would be able to concentrate on it.

She was just about to climb the stairs to the little attic retreat when the doorbell rang. Another of the town's women come to chew the fat? Erin had heard stories about the nosy, gossipy women in small towns, but she had never really believed them. Not the more extreme ones, anyway. She'd seen enough gossip in small communities and school to know that it wasn't out of the realm of possibility, but she thought the stories were exaggerations. Maybe the women of Bald Eagle Falls were the ones the stories were all about.

As she composed herself and moved toward the door to answer it, the doorbell rang again, followed by a hard rap of knuckles. Someone was certainly impatient to talk to her!

Erin opened the door and found herself face-to-face with Officer Terry Piper. For a moment, she was disoriented. She had only ever seen him downtown at the shop, so it seemed out of character for him to come to her house. But of course, they were only a few blocks apart and the police department for Bald Eagle Falls probably covered a wide geographic area, expanding outward to include the more rural homes around the town as well.

"Officer Piper. I didn't know you were coming."

He nodded. K9 panted at his side. Erin just looked back at him.

"Can I come in, ma'am? I have some more questions for you."

"I was hoping... that you were just here to tell me that I could go back to my bakery. Have the police released the scene?"

"Not yet, I'm afraid. Probably by the end of the day. It's not a big area, there's not that much to search."

Erin reluctantly stepped back to let him in. What else could he have to ask her about? She had already told him everything she could think of with regard to finding Angela's body. As he'd said, it was a small area. There wasn't that much to tell. She went down the stairs, turned the corner, saw the body. By that time, it was too late to do anything for Angela. The opportunity for intervention was long gone.

Piper came in, wiping his feet on the mat. The dog was quiet at his side, well-behaved, though looking around and sniffing the air eagerly, gathering information about the unfamiliar surroundings. Piper raised his eyebrows and Erin directed him to the couch, sitting across from him in a Queen Anne chair.

"Have you found anything?" she asked. "I mean, it's probably too early to have tested any of the food for wheat ingredients, if they were contaminated at the warehouse."

K9 made a grumbling noise as he lay down at Piper's feet. He would, Erin was sure, much rather have done some further investigating, sniffing out all her secrets.

"Yes, they have to be sent to a lab in Memphis. They've all been bagged and tagged and sent over on a rush. But it will be a few days before we hear anything back."

"You have a courier to Memphis?" Erin hadn't seen any courier companies around town, though she supposed one of them might have a drop box somewhere. Or would they make a special trip to pick something up for the police department?

"We sent a contractor with all the evidence that needed to be tested. You don't need to worry, everything is sealed. It can't be tampered with."

Erin hadn't even thought of that. She gave it a little consideration before she decided that it really was nothing to worry about. They had special procedures and protocols. Ways to ensure that the chain of evidence was maintained.

"So... what did you want to ask me about? I haven't thought of anything else that would be helpful to you."

"How much did you know about Mrs. Plaint's allergy?"

"Nothing. I didn't know anything about it until she told me at the counter that day."

"Exactly what did she say to you?"

"Exactly?" Erin closed her eyes and tried to conjure it up. "She said... she had a very severe allergy to wheat. She was worried about if I used any wheat at all in the bakery. She said she would know if I did. She'd be able to tell." Erin opened her eyes and looked at him. "She was sort of intimidating. But I know how it is with people with severe reactions... they have to stand up for themselves and sometimes act like a bit of a bully... because people don't understand or won't believe that they have a life-threatening condition."

"Why wouldn't they?"

"Because other people adopt special diets as fads and they don't really keep them, or are casual about them. Someone who says they are allergic to gluten and then picks at the pasta on the plate of the person next to them. Or order beer. People who think that it will help them to lose weight. Or just that it's a healthy thing to do for one reason or another, but they're willing to bend the rules. So then servers and restaurant owners think it doesn't really matter. They think that everyone who comes into the store with 'allergies' is just being a pain in the neck and they won't react if there's a questionable ingredient or cross-contamination."

"Did Mrs. Plaint tell you that she had an…" Piper pulled out his notepad and referred to it. "An autoinjector?"

"No… not that I recall. Gema Reed was by here earlier and she said that Angela had one. She said that everyone knew about it, that Angela told them how to use it if she had an attack."

Piper gazed at her for a moment, considering this, then made an additional note in his pad. "It's interesting that you would offer that information."

Erin shifted uncomfortably. "What do you mean? You asked me about her autoinjector. That's all that I know about it. I didn't hear anything from Angela. Just from Gema, today."

He rubbed the space between his lip and his nose.

"Why didn't Angela use her autoinjector?" Erin said with sudden realization. "Didn't she have time to realize that she was having a reaction? Or was it faulty? Did she use it and it didn't help?"

He held up his hands to stop her from asking further questions. "She didn't have an autoinjector on her person."

"What? But Gema said that she had one. That she told people how to use it."

"And when she needed it, not only was there no one there to help her, but she didn't even have it with her."

"But that doesn't make sense. Gema said that Angela has had a number of close calls. If she knew she was that sensitive and she had had close calls in the past, why wouldn't she have it on her?"

"We've looked for it. We've checked every inch of the bakery, in case she dropped it and it rolled under something. But no luck. It isn't there."

Erin covered her mouth, horrified. Angela wouldn't have left it in her other purse or pants. She wouldn't have left it at home just once. Or in her car. She knew she was going into a bakery, potentially a hot zone for contamination. Surely she wouldn't have walked into a bakery without making sure her autoinjector was handy. Or two. A lot of people carried two, in case the first wore off before an ambulance could get there. With how far Bald Eagle Falls was from a major hospital, she might have even had a stockpile of them, to last her however long it would take to get her to proper medical care.

"She wouldn't have gone anywhere without an autoinjector. Especially not into a bakery."

"You said that you didn't know her that well and had never talked to her about her autoinjector."

"And that's all true. But would you? If you knew you were deathly allergic to wheat, would you walk into a bakery without one?"

"Maybe into a gluten-free bakery. It was supposed to be safe."

"But she didn't know that beforehand. She didn't know whether I catered to multiple special diets—like I do—and only some of the product was gluten-free. She could have been walking into a cloud of flour dust hanging in the air."

"And that would have been enough to trigger her allergy?"

"From what everybody has said, it would have."

K9 let out a big sigh, breaking the tense atmosphere. Erin laughed and Piper allowed a tiny crack in his facade, one corner of his mouth curling into a dimple. He nudged K9 with his toe.

"Decorum, partner. Maintain an appearance." He looked at Erin. "He prefers foot patrol to the cerebral stuff."

"I can understand his point. He doesn't know why he has to come sit here and listen to us talk. He doesn't understand what happened to Angela."

Piper nodded. He rose to his feet, tugging his heavy belt up a little. K9 jumped eagerly to his feet.

"You'll let me know when I can go back to my shop?" Erin asked. "I'm really anxious about having to stay closed today. The day after opening… it's not good for business. And I'll have a ton of baking to do before I can open tomorrow, if it's been cleared. I can't just open without anything to sell."

He nodded. "You do all the baking yourself? No assistant?"

"I'll need to get someone before too long. Even if it's just an after-school student to take care of the till. Otherwise, I'll burn out."

As soon as Officer Piper told her she could go back to the shop, Erin was there. Almost before she even got off the phone with him. He rolled his eyes when she arrived there before he was finished removing the police tape from the front and back doors.

"Ready to get cookin'?" he inquired.

"More than ready." Erin looked at her watch. "But only for a couple of hours, because I have to be up early in the morning. That's assuming that everything was left clean in here?" She unlocked the front door of the shop.

"There may be some fingerprint powder to wipe down, I don't think there's anything else to worry about."

"And what was removed from the scene, other than samples of my baking?"

"Small amounts of ingredients. We didn't take the whole bags, just a sample to test for contamination."

"Okay. Thanks."

She hurried into the shop and locked the door behind her, not wanting Piper or anyone else to interrupt her. She didn't have a lot of time and she didn't want to talk to anyone.

Her sensitive nose picked up on a chemical smell that still hung in the air. She wondered what they had used and what they had been testing for. She was pretty sure that fingerprint powder wouldn't leave any detectable scent. She remembered K9 sniffing the air at her house. Would it be a blessing or a curse to have a nose as sensitive as a dog's? She always regretted hers when there was something noxious in the air. Other people seemed to be able to ignore it, but Erin would have to leave the room gagging. She'd always been that way. Probably no one else would even notice the chemical odor.

The chemical smell would be gone by morning, replaced by the smells of chocolate, vanilla, and fresh-baked bread. There could be nothing better.

The fingerprint powder was all over everything. The display case where little Peter had pressed his hands and face into the glass to look at the baked goods. The wall. The chrome around the glass case. The steel countertop. The door handles. Everything. Deciding she didn't have the time to go downstairs to see what state the basement had been left in, Erin just locked the door and took down the placard. If anyone wanted to use the facilities, they would have to try a different store. She didn't need any ghouls snooping around in the basement, trying to identify the exact spot Angela had died in. She would keep public access to the stairs locked until interest had petered out and she'd had a chance to do a thorough cleaning.

There were a couple of muffin batters in the fridge, so Erin started by pouring those into paper liners and throwing them in the oven. She had a sourdough as well and took a portion to shape into loaves, getting those started. While the muffins baked, she quickly wiped down all the fingerprints she could find and then started on some cookie dough. She would use the same base mixed with several different add-ins to cut down on the prep time required for a variety of cookies.

She hadn't put her earbuds in, working too quickly to even stop to do that, so she heard the noise at the back door, quiet though it was. Erin froze, elbow deep in a vat of bread dough, and listened.

It was just a tree branch rubbing against the outside of the building.

Or something equally innocuous.

Though she tried to make herself get back to work, she couldn't focus on her work, trying to hear what was going on. *Was somebody trying to pick the lock of the back door?* They had to be able to see the lights on in the bakery and know that someone was there.

Or was that part of the plan? Maybe it was someone who wanted her to be there. Someone who wanted her out of the way. She had thought that Angela was her only real antagonist. The competition. But what if there was someone else? Someone who had previously picked the lock or used some other method to get into her bakery. The entity who had broken her mug and shifted the papers in her office.

It was just paranoia. Anxiety. Because Erin was tired and because she was involved in a police investigation of an unexpected death. Her imagination was getting away from her.

Erin determinedly went back to kneading her bread. Though, since gluten-free bread doughs were more liquid than gluten bread dough, it was really just mixing rather than kneading.

The noise continued. Eventually, Erin's anxiety subsided. No one was going to take fifteen minutes to pick the lock of an occupied shop and keep at it. It had to be a branch rubbing against the building, like she had initially thought. Or just the building itself making noises.

After it ceased to be anxiety-producing, it became an irritant. She should just put her earphones in and keep working, but she would know, even with music on, that the noise was still there. She'd have to keep taking the earphones out to check one more time whether it was still there.

She hadn't heard the noise other days that she had been there.

And there hadn't been a wind when she had arrived at the shop.

With an angry breath out, Erin extricated herself from the dough, scraped it off of her hands and arms, and washed up. She wiped sweat from her forehead and went to the back door. The door to the stairs was open. She closed it, irritated that the police had left it sitting open. She didn't want to have her attention drawn to the basement.

The scratching at the door resumed. Erin stood there for a moment, breathing shallowly and staring at the back door.

It was low on the door. Animal-like. She was sure it would just be a branch.

She unlocked the door and tentatively pushed the door open a few inches to have a look.

There was a movement, a silhouetted shape in the dimness, that made Erin gasp and jump back.

And then a dirty little head thrust through the door, and a slim, lithe shape followed it into the shop.

A cat.

A little, bedraggled, mostly-orange kitten.

"Oh, my goodness." Erin let out another breath. "Where did you come from?"

The kitten looked up at her and meowed silently. Something too ultrasonic for her to hear.

"You must be a stray. It doesn't look like anyone has been taking care of you."

The little cat rubbed against her legs, but when Erin moved toward it, it took off, streaking away from her.

"No you don't! I don't want a cat in here. Come on. Out you go." She pushed the door open wider and went after the cat, trying to shoo it back out of the shop. "Out, out, out! No animals in my bakery."

The cat avoided her, moving much faster than she would have thought possible, and wedged itself back behind the fridge. Erin was afraid to move the fridge in case she hurt it. After considering the situation for a few minutes, she decided to leave the door open, and the cat would eventually wander out and leave the shop once she was occupied with something else. It was only afraid of her because she had chased it.

She went back to work, keeping an eye out for the kitten. It stubbornly stayed out of sight. Erin looked at her watch. It was getting late and she knew she had to be heading home. She covered up the loaves of bread and cleaned up the various mixing bowls. As she put away milk and eggs, a little head poked out inquisitively from under the fridge.

"Well, hello," Erin murmured to it.

The kitten mewed and came out from under the fridge. It again rubbed against her legs and this time Erin did not try to pet it. She continued to put things away, ignoring the kitten. It became gradually bolder, not flinching away whenever she moved. Erin took the garbage out to the back lane, expecting the kitten to follow her out the door. But the perverse little creature didn't. It just sat in the kitchen waiting for her to come back.

"It's time for you to go," Erin told the cat firmly.

The cat tilted its head and looked at her.

Erin went to the fridge and looked over the contents. The cat watched as she got the carton of eggs back out again, then got out a saucer and cracked the egg into it. It meowed and wound itself around her ankles.

Erin whisked the egg with a fork and bent over to hold it close to the kitten. "You see that?" she asked. "You smell that? You're hungry, aren't you?"

The cat meowed eagerly, following the saucer. Erin moved slowly, not wanting to scare it away. It followed the saucer closely, sniffing at the air and occasionally standing up on its hind legs to try to get a better look. She walked out the back door. For a moment, the kitten stayed inside the warmth and shelter of the kitchen, but it was drawn by the smell of the egg and eventually followed her out. Erin put down the saucer. The kitten hovered close by, not approaching while she was still too close. Erin moved back to the door of the shop and the kitten closed in on the saucer, bending down to sniff and then to lap at the raw egg. Erin stepped back into the shop and closed the door.

Erin unlocked the front door of the bakery, her stomach tied in knots with her anxiety that she wasn't going to get any business. The lost day meant that she didn't have any momentum. People would be afraid her goods were contaminated. Or they wouldn't want to eat somewhere that someone had died. Or they would decide not to frequent her establishment out of loyalty to the deceased. There were so many reasons for people to avoid going to Auntie Clem's and few she could think of for them to go.

But there were already a few people waiting outside the door. Erin smiled and greeted them and went back behind the counter to serve them.

"I just can't believe about Angela," Melissa said, after Erin had served the first two customers, who had been tactful enough to avoid the topic. "Who would ever have thought that such a thing could happen?"

"I'm told she had had several bad reactions before," Erin offered, trying to keep her face pleasant and not rise to Melissa's tendency toward drama.

"Well, I know, but *here*, of all places!"

"It's possible that she had developed a new allergy. That happens sometimes, you know, especially once you have one severe reaction. She might have been allergic to something she had never had a reaction to before. Another ingredient in the muffins, or something in the air or something she touched. It could have been nothing to do with the muffins or the shop. Maybe she took a cough drop or some other medication. We don't know anything yet about what she actually reacted to."

"That's a very positive way to look at it, I'm sure." Melissa looked around at the other customers and leaned closer to Erin. "Have you seen the paper this morning?"

"No. I thought the paper came out Thursdays?"

"They did a special print run today. Because of breaking news."

Erin wasn't so sure she wanted to know what the breaking news was. In fact, she was sure she didn't want to know.

"Did you want a muffin this morning?" she asked Melissa. "Maybe some rustic bread for supper tonight?"

But Melissa wasn't even looking at the baked goods in the display case or at the price board. She was digging around in her oversized shoulder bag. The businessman behind her was shifting impatiently and Erin made a show of looking around Melissa at him.

"Could I help you, sir?"

He smiled and stepped forward beside Melissa to make his breakfast selection. Erin rang up his order, ignoring Melissa, and looked to the next person in line. She saw Peter and his mother. She had the baby in a sling again, but the two little girls were not with them. Peter eagerly stepped forward to point out which muffin he wanted. His mother bent in close to Erin.

"Peter didn't have any reactions," she said.

Erin blinked at her. She smiled tentatively. "That's good," she said. "I'm glad to be able to provide products that he can eat…"

"What I mean is… there couldn't have been any gluten in the cookies or bread, or Peter would have had a reaction. I don't think any of your food is contaminated."

Erin breathed out in relief and gave her a more genuine smile. "Thank you for that. I've been worried about what people would think. I'm sure there are all kinds of rumors going around about what happened and the people who really need the bakery will end up avoiding it."

The bells over the front door jingled several times. Erin looked up. The bakery was getting rather busy. Even busier than on opening day, when she had offered complimentary cookies and muffins. She didn't recognize all the faces as people who had been there before. A lot of people who normally went to Angela's bakery must have decided to try out Auntie Clem's instead. Gema had said that Erin no longer had any competition. Angela's bakery must have closed with her death, which was odd if she was the owner but didn't actually work out of the bakery herself. Wouldn't her business keep operating until it was transitioned to a new owner?

Erin settled up with Peter's mother, her mind elsewhere. Then Melissa had finally sorted out what she was looking for in her bag and thrust the slim little town newspaper in front of Erin's face.

"There! That's what I'm talking about."

Erin pulled back slightly to look at the big black headline.

POLICE DETERMINE ANGELA PLAINT'S DEATH A HOMICIDE.

Chapter Six

ERIN'S MIND IMMEDIATELY FLASHED back to the questioning by Piper about what Erin knew of Angela's allergies and autoinjector.

Auntie Clem's no longer had any competition.

Did Piper really think that Erin would murder the competition? What kind of person would jump from having a discussion about the competition between the two bakeries to murdering her opposition? Even if Piper interpreted the sidewalk collision between the two women as a physical altercation, what would make him think Erin was capable of murder?

"Are you okay?" Melissa asked.

Erin blinked. She had customers. She didn't have time to be panicking about Terry Piper's speculations. She smiled at the next person in line behind Melissa.

"Can I help you?"

Melissa still didn't move away from the counter or choose a muffin. Erin continued to serve customers while Melissa tried to engage her in conversation.

"Can you believe it? Murder?"

"No," Erin snapped. "I can't believe it. Why would he think it was murder? It was obviously just an allergic reaction. An allergy. No one could have predicted it."

"Someone could have caused it," Melissa countered. "It could have been malevolent. Contaminate something that

Angela had with wheat. Steal her autoinjector. It would kill her as surely as a bullet between the eyes. In fact, it did."

Erin counted cookies into a bag, and then had to go back and count them again to be sure she had the right number.

"But why? If it was murder, then someone had to have motive. Who had motive to kill her? And who could have gotten close enough to her to steal her autoinjector? I don't see how it could be anything other than a tragic accident. She left her autoinjector at home. She ended up reacting to something she didn't know she was allergic to. End of story."

"It was the end of the story for Angela," Melissa agreed, her dark eyes glittering. She folded the paper and put it back into her bag. "And the police determined that she did not leave her autoinjector at home. Or in her car. It is missing."

"Officer Piper told the newspaper that it wasn't at her house?"

"Officer Piper wrote it in his official report. The report that he gave to the coroner in the city."

"How would you know that?"

"Because I do transcription for the police department."

Erin closed her mouth before she could blurt out a comment about police reports being confidential. That would be shooting herself in the foot if she wanted Melissa's insight into the investigation. Erin rang up the next order and collected the customer's money.

"She could have dropped the autoinjector somewhere. Officer Piper can't search the entire town."

"He doesn't think so. He thinks it was intentionally taken from her to prevent her from saving herself from a fatal reaction." Melissa looked at Erin expectantly.

Erin sighed. "I could never do something like that. It would take someone pretty sadistic to take away her autoinjector and just watch her choke to death."

Melissa looked thoughtful. "They didn't necessarily watch her," she pointed out. "They could have taken it before she had a reaction. Or left before she died."

"This is morbid." Erin took a breather while the next customer stared at the display case, mulling over her choices. "If he thinks it's murder, he doesn't think someone just happened to take her autoinjector and then she just happened to have a reaction and needed it. He thinks..." Erin swallowed. "He thinks that someone intentionally took her autoinjector and caused a reaction. Or caused a reaction and took her autoinjector."

"You?"

"Did he... name me in his report? As a suspect?"

"Not in the report to the coroner."

Erin let out a sigh of relief. She put blueberry muffins in a box, smiling at her customer, a wrinkled little Asian woman with cherry cheeks and sparkling eyes. The sweet vanilla smell of the muffin filled her nose.

"But he *does* name you in his report to the Sheriff." Melissa smiled broadly, as if Erin should be proud of herself for being a prime murder suspect.

"How could he think I had anything to do with it? I can understand him thinking that she was the victim of accidental cross-contamination of something she bought here. But murder? I don't have a motive, I only just met the woman!"

"You are competitors for the town's business."

"Competitors don't kill each other!"

The next customer in line was Mary Lou Cox, looking as coiffed and put-together as always. "I gather you've heard the news," she said in a low, sympathetic voice.

"I was just filling her in." Melissa gave Mary Lou's arm a conspiratorial nudge. "Isn't it awful news about Angela?"

"Worse news for Erin than for Angela. Angela is dead whether it was an accident or homicide. But for Erin to be implicated in the crime..." Mary Lou *tsked* and shook her head. "You're the one I feel sorry for."

"I can't believe anyone could think I would kill her!"

"How about a dozen assorted cookies?" Mary Lou suggested, peering into the display case. "That would be a nice treat for a couple of hardworking boys, don't you think?"

Erin nodded and started putting cookies into a bag.

"Only don't give me a baker's dozen. Just twelve. Thirteen doesn't split evenly and they'll give me all kinds of grief."

Erin smiled. "You could eat the thirteenth and they wouldn't know any better."

"Oh, no." Mary Lou smoothed her pantsuit. "Straight to the hips! I have to watch so carefully."

"How are the boys?" Melissa asked. "And Roger?"

"Just about the same." Mary Lou gave a tranquil smile. "You know, every day above ground is a good one."

Erin realized that she knew little or nothing about the families of the women she had met. As a businessperson, she would do well to learn about their families and their tastes, so she could make recommendations and build a close working relationship. It sounded mercenary, but she needed to get out of her comfort zone and ask people about themselves and their loved ones if she wanted to grow her business.

"How old are your boys?" she asked, unintentionally cutting Melissa off.

"Teenagers, fifteen and seventeen. They both have part-time jobs and work hard to contribute to the household. And working keeps them out of trouble."

"Great!" Erin too had started working young. She had known that she was going to have to support herself once she aged out of foster care, so she started earning her own income as soon as she could. "And your husband? Roger, is it? What does he do?"

Mary Lou and Melissa exchanged glances.

"He's… not been well," Mary Lou said eventually. "But we're hoping he's on the upward climb."

"I'm sorry to hear that." Erin waited, unsure of whether Mary Lou wanted to share what illness her husband was suffering from, but Mary Lou didn't say and Erin was afraid to ask. "I hope he gets better soon."

Both ladies nodded.

"Did you get anything?" Mary Lou asked Melissa, taking a step toward the door. It was plainly her intention to walk Melissa out. Erin could have hugged her.

Melissa scanned the display. Erin was pretty sure by now that Melissa had never planned to buy anything. She had just come in to gossip and see what Erin's reaction would be to the news that she was a murder suspect. "How about one of those trail mix muffins. They look good." Melissa examined her muffin while Erin rang up the purchase. "Does it have nuts in it? It seems like everyone is allergic to nuts these days."

"No, no tree nuts, no peanuts. A few kinds of seeds, dried fruit, and chocolate chips. Very power-packed, great for hikes or a post work-out meal."

Melissa patted her belly. She wasn't fat, but she wasn't as slim as Mary Lou or Erin. "I won't be hiking anytime soon. I apologize to my body in advance."

Mary Lou chuckled and the two of them left together. Erin turned her attention to the next customer in line. It was shaping up to be a busy day.

At the end of the day, Erin went out her back door to the little two-stall employee parking pad. She usually parked in front of the store, but she supposed she should start parking in back instead, leaving the space in front open for customers. There wasn't a lot of parking on Main and sometimes people had to walk a few blocks to get where they were going. And what was pleasant on a winter day would become unbearable in the summer. Though, at least, the sidewalk was shaded by the little roofs extending from the storefronts.

But would she still be there when summer came around? With the position she was in, was it wise to be planning that far ahead?

Surely nothing could come from Officer Piper's suspicions. They were baseless. He would have to come up with some proof before they were in any position to arrest Erin, let alone find her guilty in a trial.

It was bound to just fade away. She shouldn't pay it any mind. Officer Piper and Melissa could think what they liked. Erin knew she hadn't done anything wrong and anyone who knew her would know she hadn't done anything wrong.

Except, no one in town knew her at all.

She looked down at the empty saucer her little furry visitor had licked clean. She looked around, but couldn't see any sign of the kitten. She stopped herself from calling out to it. She didn't want a kitten. Especially not anywhere near the store and the baking. It was a health hazard. And someone might be allergic, reacting if they were even in the same room as the little ragamuffin. She didn't want a cat at the bakery. Someone else could take care of the stray.

She went back into the kitchen with the saucer, shutting the back door firmly behind her.

Five minutes later, she was back in the parking lot, a little kitten kibble in the saucer. She had noticed it in Clementine's pantry—in her pantry—after breakfast that morning. What would it hurt to feed the cat outside? Just to make sure that it had some source of healthy food?

She just wouldn't let it into the shop.

"Kitty, kitty, kitty?" she called softly. What was the point in calling the cat? Cats never came when they were called and this one was a stray, maybe feral. It didn't have any idea why she was making those funny noises. She shook the saucer, hoping the cat would be able to interpret the sound as food.

She had just about given up when she saw a little orange and white face peer around the corner of the fence.

"Kitty, kitty?" She shook the dish again.

The cat slunk around the yard, close to the fence, not approaching her directly across open ground. It watched her, slowing its approach as it got closer. Erin stepped back, giving it a little more space.

"Kitty, kitty? Come on little kitty. Aren't you hungry?"

It shied away at her voice, but when Erin didn't do anything threatening, it approached the saucer. It sat down and looked at the food from a few feet away. The kitten looked at Erin and mewed softly.

"It's okay. I'm not going to do anything to hurt you. Have something to eat, little fella. You must be starving. You're so skinny."

The cat watched her for a few more minutes, then covered the rest of the ground to the bowl and sniffed at the food. It started to eat.

Erin wondered if the chunks of kibble would be too big for the little cat. It was really no more than a kitten. Probably barely weaned. Or maybe the mama cat was still around somewhere, but not feeding it as often, pushing it to go out into the world to fend for itself.

But it seemed to be managing the adult cat food just fine.

"Miss Price?"

Erin looked up from the cat. Officer Piper was coming down the back lane.

"I knocked on your front door, but I couldn't get your attention. I thought something might be wrong..."

As he came to the end of the short fence, Erin saw K9 at his side. Before she could anticipate it, K9 saw the kitten and lunged, letting out a volley of barks. The kitten ran straight up Erin's pant leg, its little claws piercing and scratching through her clothes like needles. Piper reacted quickly and was able to catch K9's collar to restrain him, but the cat was already on the move.

"Ow, ow, ow!" Erin tried to catch the kitten to pull it off, but it went behind her back and, the harder she tried to reach it, the more it dug in its claws, ripping up the skin on her back and shoulders. "Oh, ow! Settle down, kitten. It's okay, he won't hurt you. He can't get you. Ow!"

Piper looked suspiciously like he was suppressing a smile. "Can I help you, Miss Price?"

"Just get that dog out of here!" Erin snapped "Get him away! It's not going to relax until the dog is gone."

"I could catch it and get it off…" He took a step forward to help.

K9 growled and pulled to get closer to the tasty morsel.

"He just wants to say 'hi,'" Piper said. "He likes other animals."

"For dinner? Don't come any closer. Take him out of here."

Piper stood there for a moment, looking for another solution. Then he shrugged. He walked away, hauling on K9's collar, and was soon out of sight and earshot.

"Okay, little guy," Erin coaxed. "He's gone now. Big mean doggie is gone. You can let go. Come on…"

No matter how she twisted and squirmed, she couldn't get her hands behind her back to capture the frightened kitten. It nimbly avoided every effort.

"Big mean doggie?" Piper repeated.

Erin turned to see him return, without the dog this time. He held up his hands.

"No big mean doggie," he assured her. "Now can I help you?"

Erin suppressed the desire to snap at him and remind him that it was his fault she was in the situation in the first place. But he was trying to help. He was trying to make up for it. She turned her back to him and held still while he approached and unstuck the kitten one claw at a time. Once she felt herself free, Erin turned back to face him.

Piper stood there, a slight dimple in one cheek, holding the terrified kitten to his chest, stroking it gently to calm it. The combination of the handsome officer in uniform and his gentleness with the helpless ball of fur just about melted Erin into a puddle right there.

"Thank you."

"To serve and protect. That's my job."

"Well, I doubt you spend all day rescuing kittens. Or maidens in distress."

"That wouldn't be half bad."

Erin took a deep breath and let it out again in a sigh.

"I didn't know you had a cat," Piper said.

"Well, I don't. Not really."

He raised an eyebrow questioningly.

"Say hello to my ghost," Erin explained. "I think it must have gotten into my bakery one night and knocked the coffee mug off the counter."

"It?" Piper repeated. "Ginger cats are usually male." He drew the kitten away from his chest for a moment, peeled back the tail for a look, and nodded. "Male."

"*He,* then," Erin amended. "I apologize for disparaging his manhood. He must have gotten into my shop."

"You know if you feed him, he'll just keep coming back. You'll never be rid of him."

"The poor thing is starving. I'll feed him until he's tamer and then... I don't know. Find a home for him."

"We've got him now. No point in waiting until he's been tamed. You want me to take him to the pound?"

"Bald Eagle Falls has a pound?"

"Well, it's really just Doc Edmunds, the vet. If he has an empty kennel or two. He'll keep it—him—for a few days, see if anyone wants him."

"And then what?"

Piper raised both eyebrows and sighed. "Not much market for stray kittens in a town like Bald Eagle Falls. Everybody who wants one has one and the rest end up prey or motor vehicle statistics. Doc Edmunds' way is kinder."

"No, I couldn't do that," Erin protested. She reached for the kitten. "Give him to me. I'll find him a home."

He didn't relinquish the kitten. "What are you going to do? If I give him to you and you take him back into your bakery, you have to put him down to get ready to go home. Then you can't catch him again."

"I tempted him out with an egg yesterday... but he still wouldn't let me touch him."

"Go get your stuff together. Lock up. Meet me at your car with a towel."

"A towel?"

"You have one, don't you? A dishtowel?"

"Yes..."

He headed out of the yard with the kitten.

"You can just walk through the bakery, you don't have to take the long way around."

"If I go inside, he's going to try to get away again. Trust me. Right now I'm the only protection he can see. Inside, there's lots of places to hide. He'll go nuts trying to escape."

"Okay... I'll see you in a minute."

Erin obeyed his instructions, gathering together what she needed and locking up. She met Piper beside her car with the dishtowel.

"Now what am I supposed to do with this?"

"Give it to me."

Erin handed him the towel. He put it over the kitten, still held at his chest. Then, as Erin watched, he began to wrap it around the kitten, until it was swaddled, little face peering out at them, all cozy and protected and unable to move.

"Did you hypnotize him?" Erin asked, looking at the motionless cat. She expected it to be frantic all wound up like that, trapped. He should be frantic, squirming and trying to wriggle free. Erin didn't have a lot of experience with cats, but she knew they could wriggle free of just about anything. "I've heard some people can hypnotize them."

"No special powers," Piper assured her. He handed her the wrapped bundle. "Just put him on your seat for the drive home. It isn't far, he'll be okay. Don't unwrap him until you're in your house. In the room you want to release him in. You might want to put him in the bathroom with a litter box, until you're sure he has the hang of it."

"You seem to know a lot about kittens."

"We always had cats around growing up. It was always a lot easier to take them to the vet wrapped in a towel than in a cage. Have you ever tried to put a cat in a cage?"

"No."

His expression was deadpan. "I wouldn't recommend it."

Erin laughed. She sat down in her car and put the kitten on the other bucket seat. "Well, thank you for rescuing me, Officer Piper. And our little friend. That really was above and beyond."

His expression became sober. He leaned in to talk to her. "I still need to talk to you. There's no point in trying to do it now, you'll just be distracted by the little furball. Could I arrange a time for you to come in to the police department for a chat?"

Erin didn't answer right away. She looked at the kitten. "Am I really a suspect, then? In Angela's murder?"

"We have some more questions."

"You really think it was murder?"

"Everyone who knew Mrs. Plaint agrees that she wouldn't go anywhere without her autoinjector. She kept it secure and on her at all times. There is no way it was an accident. Someone took that autoinjector from her. And there was only one reason anyone would take it away."

His eyes were hard, intense. All hint of amusement, tenderness, and friendliness were gone. Officer Piper was back on the job and Erin was his prime suspect in a homicide.

"When do you want me at the police station?" Erin's own voice sounded small and far away to her.

"This time tomorrow? After work? I know you're up late, so I don't want to impose on your evening. You're probably to bed right after dinner."

"If I manage to stay up long enough for dinner."

"Tomorrow then? This time?"

"Okay. I'll see you then."

If there was a good time to be saddled with a stray kitten, it was in the middle of a police investigation when Erin was badly in need of a distraction. Without the ginger kitten, she would have been left with her own thoughts all night, worrying about what was going to happen at her police interview the next day. As it was, she seemed to fly from one kitten exploit to another.

Was it any wonder that 'catastrophe' started with 'cat'?

She decided to take Officer Piper's recommendation and release the kitten in the bathroom. There, he decided to go straight up the plastic curtain. She was still wondering how he had managed to get his claws into the plastic when it became obvious that he couldn't get them back out. Just over her head, the cat was stuck, struggling mightily to free himself. She was afraid he was going to fall and wrench the leg that was stuck in the plastic out of joint. But he wasn't too keen to let her free him, biting and slashing when she tried to pull his tiny claws free.

He fell from above her head into the bathtub with a thud and she was sure he had knocked himself out or broken something, but he was up again almost immediately, trying to get a purchase on the curved porcelain sides of the tub to get out. He jumped, he cried, he scrabbled frantically without success. But he avoided her hands, whirling around and around the tub like an Indy 500 racer. Erin tried to pincer him from both sides at the same time or to throw a towel over him to try Officer Piper's trick, all without success.

But the thrown towel did succeed on one count. It was draped over the edge of the tub within the kitten's reach and he used it to climb out of the tub so that he was once more free. He squirmed back behind the commode and hid there, peering out at Erin, squished into such a tiny ball she could barely see him. Erin decided he was safe there and left him alone. She left the towel draped over the edge of the tub so that the kitten would be able to get in and out without mishap, and pulled the door shut behind her.

Of course, she didn't have any cat things prepared and that meant she would have to go back into the bathroom, risking letting him out if he didn't stay put behind the commode. But it couldn't be helped. It was the easiest place to clean up after him if he didn't use the litter box.

Since there was cat food in the pantry, Erin had to assume that Clementine had once had a cat and that she hadn't gotten rid of all her supplies. Perhaps she had intended to get another cat, but had ended up being too sick to take care of one. So, Erin went hunting. She didn't find any food dishes, so she just went with a couple of heavier bowls from the cupboard for food and water. Kitty litter sand was behind the door in the garage. There was a covered litter box in another corner of the garage. Erin decided to leave the cover off of it to make it easier for the kitten to get in and out of to encourage him to use it. She grabbed an old newspaper to put down on the floor around the kitty litter box to catch any sand that got kicked out. She considered covering the entire floor with paper to catch any accidents, but that was how you trained a dog, not a cat. A cat should instinctively go in the litter box.

Erin inched the door open, ready for an escape attempt. But the kitten did not try to get out and Erin was able to get in with the litter box and put it down, kicking the door shut behind her. There was still no sign of the kitten. Bending down to look, she saw that he was still squished behind the porcelain, watching her with concerned eyes. Erin left again to get the food and water dishes. His ears did perk up when he smelled the cat kibble. He watched her intently. Erin filled the water bowl and put it down.

"How about that, little guy?" Erin whispered. "Still hungry? Thirsty? You're safe here. You can come out and eat."

But she knew he wouldn't venture out. Not while she was there. It was going to take a while before he was used to her.

"Okay. See you later."

She hesitated as she left. Shut off the light or leave it on? Would he be scared of the dark? Would the light keep him awake? He didn't need the light on to see his food or the litter box, did he? Cats could see in the dark. Eventually, she decided to turn it off.

"Goodnight, kitty."

Chapter Seven

*I*F SHE THOUGHT THAT the kitten would give her a peaceful night's sleep, she had another think coming. She forewent her usual bed-time bath, deciding that might be traumatic to the kitten. She instead put on fuzzy pajamas, had a cup of tea, read a few pages in her book, and slid into bed. As soon as she closed her eyes, her thoughts went immediately to Officer Piper. And not in a good way.

But before she could worry about how anxiety was going to keep her awake all night, she was faced with a new concern.

At first she thought it was a baby crying or someone having a fight outside. But as she tried to sort out the wails, she realized that the caterwauling was, in fact, a cat. Her cat.

And it was loud enough that she was sure the neighbors could probably hear it. How could such a little animal make such a horrible racket? Erin went to the bathroom door and banged on it.

"Quiet down!"

The noise stopped.

Erin went back to her bed. Just as she was pulling up the covers, it started again. Erin listened for a moment, thinking maybe it was just one last hurrah, the kitten getting in the last word, and then he would stop.

He did not.

Erin went back to the bathroom. She opened the door and turned on the light, wondering if she would find that he was again hanging from the curtains or had gotten himself into some other fix. But he was standing in the middle of the bathroom. He immediately scooted backward and again hid behind the toilet.

"What's wrong with you?" Erin murmured to him. "Don't you know it's time to go to bed? Kittens need their sleep."

He stared up at her.

Erin reconsidered turning the light off. Cats were nocturnal, so maybe leaving the light on would signal to him that it was time to go to sleep. Or maybe if he was frightened, the light would be soothing. He was just a weanling, she reminded herself. It was probably the first night he'd been away from his mother and littermates.

Deciding that maybe he needed something comforting, Erin went to the sewing room and started looking through the fabric and craft supplies for inspiration. She cut a couple of yards of penguin-patterned fleece from a bolt and grabbed a couple of scraps of leopard-spotted faux fur. She put them into a wicker basket that was much too big for the kitten, but would be cozy when he was full-grown.

She returned to the bathroom, still opening the door with great care in case the little cat was getting more bold with all of the coming and going. He was still hiding behind the commode. With the litterbox and the food dishes, the small room was already crowded. The basket was going to make it unnavigable if she had to get up in the middle of the night. But she couldn't think of another solution.

Hoping to reduce the likelihood of a nocturnal adventure—she certainly didn't want to be chasing a kitten through the house in the middle of the night—Erin used the facility.

"Sorry," she murmured to the kitten before flushing. She was afraid he would go rocketing around the room when his hiding place was suddenly filled with the sounds of rushing water, maybe even climb her like he had when K9 put on an appearance, but he stayed put. Erin washed and dried her hands.

She crouched down and reached around the toilet. Not to get the kitten out, just to stroke him for a moment. To try to connect with the little furball and reassure him. He didn't slash at her, bite her, or back away, all of which she considered good signs.

"There, see? Everything is okay. You're safe here. No need to cry. Okay?"

She settled the basket as close to his hiding place as possible to encourage him to investigate it, left the light on for him, and headed back to bed.

All chance of sleep seemed to have fled. Her brain was in high gear. Her thoughts went again to the upcoming police interview. Surely Piper wouldn't arrest her. If they'd had anything they considered proof of her guilt, he would have arrested her that evening, not helped her to rescue the kitten. After all, she couldn't take care of a kitten while in jail.

The crying started up again. Erin looked at her clock. She would give him fifteen minutes to settle down. The neighbors couldn't report her for fifteen minutes of noise. If he continued after that, she would… check on him again and try to calm him down. It was worse than having a baby. She really didn't have any idea what to do to calm down a lonely kitten.

She lasted five minutes. Five minutes of torture. When she couldn't stand it anymore, she threw herself out of bed and stalked to the bathroom. She opened the door.

"Stop crying!"

The kitten froze in the middle of the floor, staring at her with big, liquid eyes, then all four feet were scrabbling for purchase on the slick tile floor before he managed to get moving and again dashed behind the commode. After making sure the door was shut securely behind her, Erin followed the kitten. She reached behind the toilet and got her hand around his belly. He scratched and bit, which hurt, but Erin wasn't letting him go. She carried him to the basket and put him down, holding him there firmly.

"This is where you go to sleep. You can't be up crying all night. See how nice and comfy cozy it is? Feel the fur." She stroked it with the other hand. "Just like your mama. I know it's scary, but you can be warm and safe here. You're okay. Just snuggle into this little nest and you can curl up and go to sleep."

She gradually released the pressure on the kitten's body. Once he was free, he squirmed away from her, around the side of the basket, burrowing down under the fleece. Then he hid there, turning his body in a circle so he could look up out of his burrow at her.

"That's right," Erin whispered. "Isn't that so much more comfy than hiding behind the commode? Silly kitty. Now go to sleep."

She crept out of the bathroom, watching to make sure the little kitten didn't make a break for the door. She tiptoed down the hall. Maybe if he didn't hear her walk away, he'd think she was still outside the door and wouldn't be so lonely. *Sleep, kitten.* Erin needed her sleep or it was going to be impossible to get up in the early hours to bake. She really did need to find an assistant. It wouldn't pay much, but if she could get a student to work a few hours before and after school…

She slid into bed as quiet as a mouse. But the kitten seemed to know exactly when she got herself situated. She closed her eyes and he immediately started howling again. Erin muttered a few choice words under her breath about kittens who keep people awake at night and went back down the hall.

This time she didn't open the door and go in. She just stood outside, making calming, soothing noises. The kitten quieted. Erin waited. Just as she was about to head back to her bedroom, the noise started again.

"Shh, kitty. Go to sleep. Curl up in a little furball and go to sleep in your basket…"

The noise stopped. Erin waited. She looked at her wrist, even though she wasn't wearing a watch.

She was starting to feel weepy.

She was a murder suspect.

She had to get up early in the morning. And that blasted little kitten wasn't going to let her get a wink of sleep.

She opened the door. The kitten was in the middle of the floor. He completed his skittering run behind the commode. Erin scooped him up and put him in the basket. He burrowed down under the blanket.

Erin picked up the basket and took it out of the bathroom. She considered putting it in the garage, but that would be cruel. The concrete floor was cold and there were all kinds of tools and maybe pesticides or other poisons that could kill a curious kitten. She wouldn't be able to catch him again and she was afraid she would still be able to hear him crying even all the way back in the house. She went instead back to her bedroom. She shut the door and put down the basket. Then she climbed into bed.

It was a few minutes before she could hear the kitten moving around, climbing back out of the basket. He started to cry.

"Shh, go to sleep."

He stopped. There was silence for a few more minutes. He started to cry again.

"Shh, kitty. Enough crying. You're not alone. Now go to sleep."

He quieted again. Erin listened for him. He was quiet, kitten soft paws on plush carpet. But she could still hear him every now and then as he sniffed and sneezed at various items around the room or pushed against things with his face or body. Listening to his explorations, Erin started to drift. She wasn't thinking about her police interview because she was listening too closely to the tiny noises of the kitten. She was almost asleep when he climbed up the sheets onto the bed. He crept around the bed, exploring. Erin kept absolutely still, not wanting to scare him away or to have him start chasing her wiggling toes under the bedding. If she just stayed still, he would settle in and let her sleep.

Eventually, she felt the kitten squeeze up against her back, kneading the bed with his little paws. He started to purr, a tiny, old-man grumble. His purrs and the warmth of his body lulled her to sleep.

When Erin's alarm went off in the morning, she reached over to slap it off, then lay there in the bed trying to rouse herself enough to get up and go to work. As she lay there, her mind started to work, reminding her with a sick feeling of dread of her upcoming interview with Officer Piper after work. Maybe she would stay home sick. He couldn't complain if she were too sick to make the appointment.

But she couldn't stay sick forever and, sooner or later, she would have to talk to him. It might as well be sooner. She had learned, over the years, that if she were in trouble, it was best to get it over with. Half the suffering was in avoiding punishment.

Then she remembered the kitten. She didn't move, trying to locate the critter before moving. He was so small, she didn't want to crush him rolling over.

"Kitty, kitty, kitty?" she called softly.

The pillow she was lying on shifted. Erin moved her hand up and found the kitten, his body soft and warm, lying on her pillow curled around her head.

"You silly cat!"

Erin sat up. She turned on the lamp next to the bed and looked at him. He sat up and yawned, a wide pink-tongued yawn with his eyes closed and his ears quivering back.

"You're just the cutest thing."

He didn't run away at the sound of her voice. He just sat there, looking at her. Erin reached a tentative hand out toward him, expecting him to rocket away. But he just sniffed. Not getting any closer, not backing away, just getting her scent.

"Are you actually going to let me pat you?"

She inched closer. He touched his little pink nose to her fingers and didn't pull away. Erin stroked him gently. He started to purr, pushing his head into her hand. She rubbed his head and ears and ran her fingers along his back. He stretched out on the bed and turned over, showing his belly. Erin scratched his belly and he was suddenly all claws, grabbing her hand.

"Ouch!" Erin jerked her hand back and this time he did jump away from her, scampering off the bed and hiding in the open closet. Erin sucked on one of her knuckles, bleeding from his needle-sharp kitten claws. "Ow, what did you do that for? I thought you wanted me to scratch your belly!"

He peered at her from the depths of the closet.

Erin caught sight of her clock and realized she'd better get moving. She was normally much more efficient about getting ready in the morning. Kittens slowed things down significantly.

"You can hide there all you like," she told the kitten. "As long as you find your litter box when you need it!" She headed off for the bathroom herself. Time to shower and get ready to go.

When she stepped out of the shower, the kitten was there, in the middle of the bathroom floor. He sat there staring up at her, unafraid. She was glad he hadn't held her outburst against her. As she toweled off, he rubbed against her legs, getting his fur damp. He sat and tongue-washed while she quickly combed out her hair and put on a touch of makeup. The ladies in Bald Eagle Falls did not go out in public without makeup on. But she would probably need to reapply it after working over the stove for a couple of hours.

"You're going to need a name."

He stopped licking for a moment and looked at her. Then he went back to work. She wondered whether she was going to have to give him a real bath to get all the dust and dirt out of his fur. Or whether he had fleas or mites or some other parasite. She hadn't even thought of that before letting him sleep on the bed with her. She'd been so tired she hadn't thought any of it through.

"Well, time to eat. You're going to need some breakfast too, aren't you?"

She picked up his dishes and carried them with her to the kitchen. The cat followed close behind her.

He sat in the middle of the floor and continued his grooming regimen. Any time she made an unexpected movement, whether across the kitchen to the fridge, or getting a mug out of the cupboard, or closing the door on the toaster oven to warm her bagel, he stopped what he was doing and looked at her. But he didn't run away.

Erin tended to the kitty, giving him a fresh bowl of water and putting kibble into the dish. As soon as she put the dishes on the floor, he sauntered over to have a look, as if he'd been a house pet his whole life. Erin smiled and watched him for a moment before grabbing her coffee and bagel and sitting down at the table for a quick repast before heading over to the bakery.

Chapter Eight

SHE WAS A LITTLE worried about leaving the kitten all alone in the house. She hoped that he wouldn't yowl while she was gone. Since it was daytime, he should be more interested in sleeping and, hopefully, wouldn't be looking for company. And she didn't yet know whether he would use the litter box, but didn't dare shut him in the bathroom. His cries would have the neighbors on the warpath, at the very least, if not the police called, thinking there was a baby left in the house alone. But the cat had eaten and found a patch of sunshine to lie down in. He didn't appear to be worried about her leaving. Hopefully the house would be intact when she returned at the end of the day.

Her mind was still on the kitten when she pulled into the parking lot behind the store. And on the baking she was going to need to get done before opening in a few hours. And, niggling at the back of her mind, the interview with Officer Terry Piper when she closed the shop for the day. She wondered what had really happened to Angela. How she had really ended up dead in Erin's basement.

She was not thinking about the ghost. That mystery had already been solved.

She immediately got to work on the batters she had left in the fridge. The muffins could bake while she got the ingredients for the next treat assembled. But as she started the big mixer, which ground and grumbled like the bearings were going to pop out, she caught a movement out of the corner of her eye.

She turned her head to see what it was, even though she knew it was just a shadow or a trick of a light and there was nothing to see.

But there was.

The girl froze, her eyes wild.

"Who are you? What are you doing in my store? Where did you come from?" The words tumbled out of Erin's mouth without a thought and she moved toward the girl to prevent her from leaving. Who was this, appearing in the middle of her store with both of the doors locked?

The girl was worn and rumpled. She had stringy blond hair that reached her shoulders. Erin put her at seventeen or eighteen. She looked frightened. Lost and homeless.

"I—I'm sorry." The girl attempted to navigate around Erin, heading for the door. Erin put out her arms, making herself big and preventing the girl from going around her.

"Stop. You stay there and answer my questions, or I'll call the police."

The girl stopped. Her jaw jutted and she put on a tough front. "The police in this hole? I'd be miles away before they showed up." Her voice was a little hoarse, like she had a cold. But despite the words, she didn't try to get by Erin again. Erin was sure that she could run if she really wanted to. She could shove Erin down and make a run for it. She was right, Erin probably wouldn't be able to get Piper in there until the girl was long gone. It seemed like he was always right outside her door, though, so the girl might just as easily be wrong. And it didn't look like she wanted to take the chance to find out. Better to answer questions and get out than to take a chance and not be able to escape.

"I'm... I'm Vic. Vicky. Victoria. I just... I stayed here when you were gone, to stay safe at night. It used to be empty." She looked around, giving a shrug. "Usually, you come in the front door. The bell rings. Why didn't you come in the front door this time?"

"I parked in the back. Decided to use the employee parking space. How long have you been staying here? Since before I got to town?"

Vic nodded, watching Erin carefully for her reaction. "Yeah, sorry…"

"You broke my mug, not the cat."

"The cat?" Vic shook her head. "I knocked it off in the dark getting a drink of water. I didn't mean to. I've tried to keep everything tidy, but sometimes… you notice."

"Yes. Sometimes I do. You had Melissa convinced that the bakery was haunted by my Aunt Clementine's ghost."

The girl smiled slightly at this. "I wish I was a ghost and could go through walls."

"But you can't," Erin said. "So, how did you get in here?"

She hesitated, weighing her answer. "I might have… had a key."

"A key? How did you get a key to my shop? No one else has a key."

"My aunt was friends with yours, I guess. She had a spare key."

"And you made yourself at home, camping out in my store."

"Yes."

Erin pointed at a step-stool. "Sit down."

Vic looked like she would rather run, but after a delay of a few seconds, she obeyed and sat down. She was a tall girl, slim. She perched on the chair, looking at Erin and waiting for her to say what she was going to do about Vic's breaking and entering. Or entering, anyway. Trespassing.

"You've been staying here every night. Running out the back door when you hear me come in the front."

"Yes. You get here really early."

"A baker has to be up early."

Erin attended to her ingredients. First a stray cat and now a stray girl. The world was determined to make her open late. She wouldn't have time to replace all the day-old baking. It would still be fresh enough; she'd just mark it down. People would be happy to get specialty foods at a discount. Maybe she would start a kids' cookie club. Children could have a free cookie once a day? Once a week? How often would she need to clear out old stock? She hated to have to throw anything out. Maybe a seniors' muffin club too.

"Where are you from?" she asked Vic.

"Mmm… north…" Vic temporized. She didn't offer any more details. Didn't want to be tracked down for some reason. Had she been in trouble? Were there warrants out for her arrest? She was homeless, a burglar, was it possible she was a murderer? Had she been in the bakery when Angela had died? Without meaning to, had she contaminated something in the kitchen? Batters sitting in the fridge? Flour containers sitting open? Or had she been in the basement when Angela had died? If she had her own key, she could have let herself in and hidden in the basement, thinking she was perfectly safe, since Erin was upstairs serving customers. Until Angela discovered her.

"You're not being very helpful."

"I'm sorry… I just don't want to talk about it. I wasn't… things weren't good before I got here."

"Victoria what? What is your last name?"

"Uh, Webster. Victoria Webster."

Erin went to her office and pulled out a notepad. She wrote down the name. "Is that your real name?"

Vic didn't offer a response.

"Why did you come to Bald Eagle Falls?"

"To see my aunt."

"Who is your aunt?"

But Erin already knew before Vic could answer.

"Angela Plaint." Vic's voice was quiet, almost inaudible.

"Angela Plaint is your aunt?" Erin repeated, flabbergasted.

"Yes. Well, she was. Though… she wasn't exactly friendly when I went to see her. I thought… she would help me out. But she wouldn't have anything to do with me. Wouldn't give me so much as a glass of water or put me up for the night."

"So, you decided to stay here instead."

Vic looked down. "Yeah. I'm sorry. I thought… I don't know what I thought. It was just the only place I had to go. Aunt Angela had a spare key. I thought the place was standing empty… at least I could be indoors, off of the street. Then when you brought stuff in and opened up… I was only using it at night, when you weren't here."

"Well, you can't do that. I can't have people wandering through here. Everything in the kitchen has to be kept clean and free of cross-contamination. If you brought anything with wheat in here…"

"I didn't eat anything in here," Vic promised. "I only came here to sleep and use the commode. I didn't touch anything."

"You broke my mug. You touched my papers."

"Only to see what was going on. Whether you were starting up a business or selling the place. That's all, I swear."

Erin studied the girl's flaming red cheeks. She looked terrified. And Erin understood why, too. Vic knew that anyone with sense would immediately turn her over to the police. She had motive, means, and opportunity.

Tears glistening in Vic's eyes. "I didn't do anything to hurt Aunt Angela. She was my favorite aunt. Even if she did turn me out. I know she's had a tough life. It made her a hard person. She didn't understand my—why I went to her. I guess it was a stupid thing to do. But I didn't hurt her. I'd never hurt anyone, especially not someone in my family."

"Why don't you go home?" Erin asked gently. "Why did you run away?"

If anyone could understand running away, it was Erin. How many times had she run away from her foster families?

How many times, as an adult, had she just left when a situation became fraught? Just packed up her bags and left town?

"I didn't run away. They kicked me out. I'm eighteen, they don't have to look after me anymore. And they don't want me around. I'm... a black mark against their name."

Erin gazed at the young blond. She had obviously been living rough, but she had a pretty face. She couldn't understand how anyone could turn another person out on the streets, but especially someone so obviously young and vulnerable. Didn't they know the kind of life she would be forced to live on the streets with no lifeline?

"How would you like to earn some money?"

Vic's mouth dropped open. "What?"

"Help me out today. Help me get the baking done and set up and then you can assist behind the counter. I can't pay you much, but I have some start-up capital. Tonight you can come home with me. Have a shower and sleep in a bed for once."

Vic shook her head. "Why on earth would you do that?"

"Call me crazy," Erin said with a shrug. "I've been left with nothing too many times. I'm not going to be the cause of someone else getting turned out in the street."

"Thank you. But you don't have to do that. I can... I don't know, I can work something else out."

"You don't want the job?"

Vic stared at her, her eyes still round and disbelieving. "You really want me to work for you?"

"Let's start with a day. See how it goes."

"Okay," Vic finally agreed, her voice low and hoarse. "Yeah. I'll help you."

"Good. We'd better get to work, because I'm already behind. We can talk while we work."

She got Vic to wash up and don an apron and cap and they worked side-by-side, Erin showing Vic what she needed to do so that she could get everything into the oven on schedule.

"What are you going to tell people?" Vic asked anxiously. "Please don't tell them I'm Angela's niece."

"People won't know you? You haven't visited her before?"

"No... it's been a while, I've changed a lot. I don't think anyone will recognize me. If you tell them I'm Angela's niece, they're going to think that I killed her!"

"No one is going to think that," Erin soothed. Though she knew it was probably true. People would jump all over the disaffected relative. They'd say it was because Angela had refused to help Vic, or because Vic thought she would get Angela's money. The girl wouldn't have a chance. "If you don't want me to, I won't tell. We can just let people think that you're a friend of mine from out of town."

"Yeah." Vic blew out a breath of relief. "That would be really good. Thanks."

Gema stared at Vic and shook her gray head. "Where did she come from? I haven't seen you around here before."

"This is Vic, she's helping me today," Erin said, smiling steadily.

"North," Vic offered, again providing no further detail. Erin knew what it was like not to be from anywhere particular. People didn't like it. That was one of the reasons she always added 'Maine' when people asked. People liked to have something more. They liked something identifiable, classifiable. 'North' was just too amorphous.

"She's new in town," Erin said.

Vic was looking put-together in a crisp white apron and server's hat, her hair combed and pulled back into a sleek ponytail. She had borrowed Erin's makeup to do her face before opening, Erin keeping a close eye out while she was in the commode to make sure she didn't bolt. Vic was much more polished and relaxed, looking like she was actually enjoying herself.

A breakfast of muffins and milk hadn't hurt, either.

Vic made Erin think of the cat; homeless, in need of love and nurturing, but skittish and not sure that she was safe there.

Erin walked her through the various products on offer. "If someone wants to know about ingredients, just ask me. I haven't printed up information lists yet." Erin made a mental note that she would need to do that.

It was much easier to work the counter with two people. She really should have hired an assistant before opening in the first place. She and Vic fell into a routine. Vic smiled brightly and was enthusiastic about the food. Erin felt like she had been there right from the start. And she had been, in a way.

They grabbed an early lunch when the morning rush calmed. There was plenty of bread and fixings for sandwiches.

"This is really nice," Vic said, as they both rested their feet and munched on sandwiches, the 'back at 11:30' sign up in the door. "And the food doesn't even taste like it's gluten-free. It's real good."

"Gluten-free doesn't mean it has to suck," Erin said.

"No. I guess not. All the stuff I've had before, it's always gritty and falls apart. Or it tastes like cardboard. Your baking is real nice."

"That's the rice flour. If you're going to use rice flour, it should be superfine. You should let your batters soak. And you should combine it with other, softer flours."

"Huh." Vic took another bite of her sandwich. "You can't just substitute rice flour for wheat flour?"

"No. It would be pretty horrible."

Vic was quiet, staring out the window. She had smiled a lot while serving the customers, but now her face was solemn and contemplative.

"What are you going to do?"

"About you?"

Vic nodded.

"I don't know." Erin sighed. "I don't want to get you in any trouble. I'd like to help you out. You seem like a really nice kid. But there is a police investigation going on. They're going to need to know that you were around. They'll need your statement."

"She really died right here in the building?"

"She really did. You must have known that, you would have seen the police tape up when you came back here that night. I don't know where you were when it happened, but the police will need your alibi."

"What if I don't have one?"

"That doesn't mean you did it. It just means you can't prove where you were. It's not like you had a motive." Erin bit off the words.

Vic shook her head. Erin knew it looked bad. If Piper thought Erin was suspect, he was going to be doubly suspicious about Vic.

"We have to come clean. If it comes to light that you withheld information, they won't believe anything you say."

"What are you going to do with me?"

"I think you should come to the police station with me. After closing today."

"Or else?"

"I think you should come, Vic. Don't you?"

Vic chewed slowly. Erin knew how she felt. Or she thought she did. She wasn't any too excited about going to see Officer Piper herself. Vic was just a kid, without a friend or relative to help her through. Erin knew what it was like to be all alone.

"Yeah," Vic said finally. "I guess I better. Can't run away from it."

Erin nodded. She was relieved that Vic had agreed to go on her own. She did not want to have to turn Vic in to the authorities. It was better if it was voluntary.

Piper wouldn't throw her in jail, would he? He'd see that she couldn't be responsible for Angela's death.

Erin and Vic were both slow about closing up and cleaning up, preparing the bakery for the next day. Neither one wanted to be done and on their way to the police station.

Erin told Vic about the cat and his antics of the night before, laughing at how loud he was and how worried she had been of waking the neighbors.

"He couldn't be that loud," Vic protested.

"He was! I swear, he was like a fire alarm!"

"Are you sure it wasn't a mountain lion?"

"Just an itty bitty kitten," Erin held her hands out to demonstrate the size. "Barely old enough to be on his own."

"Let me see your hands," Vic said, looking at them. Erin held her hands out tentatively, showing Vic the palms, then the backs, not sure what Vic wanted. Vic shook her head. "He sure clawed you up."

Erin looked at the scratches, nodding ruefully. "I know. Stings like heck. But he's so cute, I can't blame him for it."

They looked around the kitchen, but there was nothing left to do. It was time to go see Officer Piper.

Chapter Nine

THE POLICE STATION WAS no more than a couple of offices at the Town Hall, which was a store front just a couple of blocks down from the bakery. A receptionist for the entire Town Hall had them sit down in a couple of straight-backed chairs to wait. It was only a few minutes before Officer Piper was there to usher Erin into the office. He looked at Erin and then looked at Vic, frowning.

"What's all this?"

"This is Vic. She needs to talk to you as well."

"Vic." He studied her with his brows drawn down. "I don't know you."

"No, sir." Vic looked at the floor.

"She's been... she's..." Erin stumbled over her words. "Can we talk to you in private? I'd rather the whole town didn't know everything."

Piper looked around. The only other person there was the receptionist. But after dealing with Melissa's gossip over what was in official police reports, Erin wasn't trusting that any of the administrative staff would be any better. Piper nodded and motioned for them both to go with him. He took them into a jumbled office, shut the door, and sat down. K9 lay down at his side, grumbling just as he had when they had come to Clementine's house. Vic snickered.

"Okay," Piper said. "Explain to me who you are."

Vic looked at Erin. She licked her lips, but couldn't seem to get started. Erin felt sorry for the girl. "She's apparently

99

been sleeping at the bakery," she said. "She had a key and let herself in and out."

"You told me that no one else had a key."

"I didn't know that anyone did. I guess Clementine had given out at least one copy."

"You'd better get the locks changed if you don't know how many copies are floating around. That should have been your first order of business when you took possession. Always change the locks on a house or a business when you take possession. Helps to prevent... unexpected guests."

"I guess I should have. I never thought of it. And I never suspected that anyone was sleeping there."

"You knew someone had been there, though. I take it Vic is your ghost."

Vic nodded. "I broke the mug," she said hoarsely.

"Well, that's one mystery solved. But not the one I would really like to be solved."

Erin nodded. "You wanted me here to talk to me about... Angela's death."

"Yes. And I expected you to be alone. I don't conduct interviews in pairs. You find more out if you interview... witnesses... separately."

"I know you just asked for me. But you didn't know about Vic. No one did."

"Exactly how long have you been in town?" Piper asked Vic.

"A few weeks."

"You were here before Miss Price."

"Yes."

"Squatting at the shop before she was even in town."

"Yes."

Piper chewed the inside of his lip, studying her. Eventually, he looked at Erin.

"I know it's a lot to ask, but could I get you to wait while I interview Vic? You probably just want to go home and to bed, but I'm going to need to get her story without you in the room. And vice versa."

"Sure, yeah. Understood."

"You're okay to wait for a while? Have you had supper?"

"I can wait. But no, I haven't had supper."

"The Chinese place across the street is good. Then you're not just sitting around waiting and won't have low blood sugar when I'm ready to talk to you."

Erin thought about it. He was probably right, and she hadn't had a really good dinner for a week, always just grabbing something quick on the way to bed.

"Okay," she agreed. "You know where to find me if I'm not back when you're ready for me."

Piper looked across the desk at Vic. "We're going to be a while."

Erin felt a lot calmer after dinner at the Chinese restaurant. Piper was right about her being in better shape for a police interview once her blood sugar was stable. She had been letting herself get run down with the launch of the bakery. If she didn't eat right and take care of herself, she wouldn't be able to keep it up.

She again took her seat outside of the police department offices. Vic and Piper were still behind closed doors. Another three quarters of an hour passed before the door opened and Piper escorted Vic out. Erin smiled at Vic, who was looking tired and red-eyed.

"Okay?" she asked, putting a hand on Vic's arm.

"Yeah." Vic sniffled. "I'm fine."

Erin looked at Piper, looking for some sign of how much trouble Vic was in. Did Piper suspect her now? And if he did, that would be good for Erin. If Vic had taken Erin's place as the prime suspect, she should be happy. But she wasn't. Her strongest instinct was to protect Vic. Just like the kitten.

"You go get something to eat now," Erin suggested, pulling her wallet out of her purse to give Vic some cash. "I'll look for you over there, or back here. Okay?" She tried to meet Vic's eyes. "You're not going to run off on me, right? You need a bed for the night; I'll help you out. Introduce you to the kitten."

Vic brightened a little at this. "Yeah, I want to see him," she agreed.

"Good. Then I'll see you back here, or across the street at the Chinese place."

Vic nodded and took the money Erin offered. Piper and Erin both watched her walk out of the building and head across the street.

"You think she'll be back?" Piper asked. "You don't think she'll run?"

"I don't know. You?"

They headed back to Piper's office and sat down.

"Hard to say. I've called Tom to keep an eye on her. He'll pick her up over there. But our resources are pretty thin. Tom's not an experienced tail."

"I'm glad you didn't arrest her."

"All I have right now are suspicions. I haven't caught her breaking any laws or even caught her in a lie. You're not charging her with trespass. There's no evidence that she had anything to do with Mrs. Plaint's death. Yet."

"You don't really think she did it, do you? It wasn't like she had a motive to murder her own aunt."

"Did she talk to you about Mrs. Plaint?"

"No, not much..." Erin shook her head. "What did she say?"

"See if she'll talk to you about it. I only have the bare bones... she wouldn't say anything more to me than she had to. But it doesn't look good."

"She couldn't have intentionally killed Angela. Not that little girl."

"She's not a little girl. She's an adult. You don't know anything about her. And what you do know should be a warning to you."

Erin knew he was right logically. But her heart was overriding her head. Yes, Vic had effectively broken into her shop and squatted there without her permission. She knew the victim and they were apparently not on the best of terms. But the girl didn't seem to harbor any grudge against her aunt. She seemed open and friendly and she had a knack for customer service.

"There's more to that girl than meets the eye," Piper warned. "You're offering to take her into your home when you know next to nothing about her… not the smartest idea."

"She needs a place to stay. You don't have any shelters in Bald Eagle Falls, do you?"

"No. But we could figure something out. Have someone take her into the city. Book a room at the motel. There's no need to put yourself in a vulnerable situation. She could steal from you and disappear in the night in your car. She could slit your throat in your sleep. There are a hundred other ways she could damage or endanger you."

"Well, she's not going to, knowing that the police are already onto her, is she?"

"There's no guarantee of that."

Erin sighed. "I trust her. I know, I'm naive to do it, but I have to. I've *been* Vic too many times before. I know what it's like not to have anyone or to have anywhere to go. I know what it's like to be discriminated against for being homeless, alone, or destitute. To have to rely on little kindnesses from people who don't know anything about you. People have helped me to get where I am. I have to help Vic. I have to."

Piper stared across the desk at her, his eyes narrow, dissecting her like a scalpel, trying to uncover all the secrets she kept hidden under the surface.

"You have an interesting past, Miss Price."

She wondered how much he'd been able to find out about her. She had dropped below the radar for long periods of time. Had he been able to fill in those gaps? Or was he still looking for answers and trying to figure out what kind of a person she really was?

"There are lots of people with interesting histories."

"Did you come here because you were in trouble?"

"I came here because my aunt left me a house and a store. I've never had an opportunity like that before. I decided to take advantage of it."

"This detective who tracked you down in Maine. What did you say his name was?"

They both knew very well that she had never told him any details about the detective. "His name was Alton Summers."

"Did he get a finder's fee for tracking you down?"

"I don't know what arrangements he had with the Estate. Of course he was paid to find me. Detectives don't work for free."

"But you don't know what kind of financial arrangements were made."

"No. Why would I?"

"What proof did you give him that you were Erin Price?"

"What do you mean? I have ID."

"ID can be faked. And even if it is real, I'm sure there is more than one Erin Price in the country. In fact, I know there are, because there were other hits on the name when I looked into your background. What proof do you have that you are Clementine's niece? Or did you and the detective just decide that you would step into the role and split the profit between you?"

"I *am* Clementine's niece. There was no need for any subterfuge. He got paid whatever he had arranged with the estate. I presented myself and confirmed that I was the Erin Price they were looking for. That's it. That's what happened."

Piper leaned back in his chair, making it creak in protest. K9 raised his head to look at his master, then put it down again with an irritated huff.

"You weren't even going by the name Erin Price when the detective found you."

"No," Erin admitted reluctantly. He'd done his homework. How much did he know about her past? She couldn't be easy to track.

"In fact, you've gone by a number of assumed names."

"Yes. But not because I'm a criminal. I took the names of my foster parents, when I could. But my birth name is Erin Price. That's what's on all my papers."

"Still, I find it troubling. You're a drifter. A con artist. Moving from place to place, operating under different names, staying around for a few months, and then going on somewhere else."

"I'm not a con. I haven't conned anyone. I have moved around. But that's not a crime."

"You're not *from* Maine."

"I don't think I said I was. I never misled you. I lived in Maine before I came here."

He considered that for a moment, then shrugged. She searched his face for some sign of the friendliness and good humor she had seen when he had helped her with the kitten. But his face was an impassive mask. He was the police. He had a job. And it wasn't his job to befriend her.

"Tell me again about the day that Mrs. Plaint died."

Erin rolled her eyes and groaned. "I've gone over it before. Why do you need me to tell it again? You're trying to see if I'll tell the same story? If you can trip me up?"

"No. I have new information. I need to hear your story again, fit it all together."

Erin shook her head. "What new information?"

"There was someone else in the bakery the day of the murder. It changes everything. I need to review everything again."

"Because of Vic? But she says she wasn't there. She left when I arrived and stayed away until after you left."

"And that may or may not be true. It colors everything. I can't verify where she was. I need to work on the assumption that she was still in the building. I need to look at the whole sequence of events again."

"Okay. Fine." Erin started to outline her day, telling Piper everything she could remember.

"When did you unlock the back stairs?" he interrupted.

Erin cut herself off and let the question sink in.

"I kept the back stairs locked. I could go through the door from the kitchen to the basement while it was locked, because it wasn't a bolt, just the door handle. But to come back up from the basement to the kitchen, I needed the key. I didn't leave it unlocked, though, just opened it with the key. I kept it locked so that customers using the commode couldn't come back up through the kitchen. No traffic through the kitchen. Just me."

"So as far as you are concerned, it was locked the whole day."

"Yes. It was."

Piper said nothing. Erin thought back. She had been through that door several times. She had used her key to reenter the kitchen every time. But had it been locked, or had she only assumed that it was?

"I never unlocked it."

"But you weren't the only one with a key."

"Did Vic say she unlocked it? Why would she do that?"

"She didn't say she did. But did she? If she was going to come and go without being discovered, wouldn't it make sense to be able to get through that door quickly? Another escape route?"

"If she had a key, she could get through it. And no one could follow her unless they had a key. It would make more sense to leave it locked. A trap."

Piper nodded slowly. He made several lines of notes on the ruled yellow pad on his desk. He shuffled papers so that a sketched floor plan was in front of him. Erin watched his eyes as he studied it. Tracing possible routes through the shop. Testing her theory.

"Vic wouldn't have unlocked that door," she told him.

"If Vic didn't unlock it, and you didn't unlock it, then who did?"

Erin blinked at him. "What makes you think someone did?"

He stared at her and didn't answer for several beats. "Because it was unlocked when I arrived on the scene."

"What?" Erin frowned and shook her head. "How? Who could have unlocked it, and how? Why?"

"There are apparently more keys around than you are aware of. And you didn't change the locks when you took possession. I've been focused on who was in the bakery. Who could have gone down to the basement while Angela was there. That meant you and any customers who were there between the time Angela went down to use the facilities. Mary Lou Cox. Melissa Lee. Gema Reed. The Potters, who you were assisting—"

"The senior couple?" Erin asked. "They couldn't have gone down and up the stairs. Especially not in the time that I went back to the kitchen to check ingredients. They both had mobility issues. They couldn't have."

"As I was going to say."

"Oh. Right."

"Glad that we're agreed on that point. So the suspect pool was limited to you and the three other ladies eating at the table."

"And now Vic," Erin said.

"Yes. The back door was bolted. The back stairs were unlocked. You could have gone into the kitchen and downstairs. Any of the three ladies could have gone down the front stairs while you were in the kitchen. They all alibi each other, but people sometimes make mistakes. Remember things differently. Or collude to keep something from the police, out of ignorance or misguided loyalty."

"But now, you think there are other suspects?"

"Who else has a key?"

"I don't know. I wasn't in contact with Clementine. So it could be…" Erin trailed off, seeing the answer in Piper's eyes. "It could be anyone."

"Exactly. If you didn't unlock the back stairs, because you didn't want customers wandering into the kitchen, and Vic didn't unlock the door, because she wanted to keep open an escape route that she could prevent anyone else from taking, then who unlocked that door and neglected to lock it again? If nobody came through the kitchen to go out through the front door, then it had to be someone with a key. The back door was bolted. Not just a spring lock. It could be opened from the inside by someone who came up the back stairs, but that person could not bolt it again. Not without a key."

Erin supposed she should be happy the suspect pool had opened up. That took some of the police suspicion off of her. With everyone who might have had a key having had opportunity to sneak down the stairs to murder Angela, Piper would have to focus his attention on those who had motive to harm her. Which put the focus back on Erin. Or maybe on Vic.

"Have you found anything out about the food that was tested?" Erin asked. "Was there any cross-contamination? It's still possible that it was just a tragic accident. Angela might have forgotten her autoinjector. Or used it and not gotten a new one yet."

"So far, nothing from the bakery has tested positive for wheat."

"Well, that's good! I mean, for my business. You can confirm that my products aren't unsafe. So the public won't avoid buying from me for fear of contamination."

"That also means it was intentional poisoning. If the wheat didn't come from the muffins, where did it come from?"

"I was wondering if she might have another allergy she didn't know about. To… chocolate, or eggs, or something else in the muffin. Or even something in the air down there. Dust or spores. Fumes from the paint thinner I used to clean the brushes."

"How likely is that?"

"You'd have to ask the coroner, I guess… I don't know if they have any way of telling whether it was wheat or some other allergen. I don't even know if they can tell the difference between something that was ingested and something that was inhaled."

"You really want this to be an accident."

"Well… yes. Of course. I don't want to be the suspect in a murder investigation. I just want to run the bakery."

He gave a thin smile. Not the kind that made the dimple appear in his cheek. No real humor behind it.

"Like I told Vic. Don't leave town."

"I don't intend to." Erin looked at her watch. "I'd really like to get home and get to bed. After making sure the kitten hasn't destroyed the house, of course."

She gave a little laugh and waited for him to join in and ask her how the kitten was and how it had settled in. But he didn't. He looked through his notes, mouth pulling down.

"Keep yourself available for further questions. I'm not done with you, but I'm going to need to go through everything again. There is still the possibility that Vic was still in the shop at the time that Mrs. Plaint was killed. And relatives… it's a fact that family is more likely to have killed her than a near-stranger."

"So, she's a better suspect than I am."

"That should make you happy."

"It should, but it doesn't. I feel bad for Vic. She didn't do it."

"You leave that to me."

She walked out of Officer Piper's office feeling disappointed and depressed. A lot of it was probably just attributable to being tired. She always got more emotional when she was tired. 'Things will look better in the morning' had long been a late-night mantra for her. And things always did look better once she was rested.

She should have been happy there was a better suspect than she was. She should have been happy that Piper was considering outsiders. Anyone else who might have a key to the bakery. And she should have been happy that he hadn't arrested her for anything.

But she didn't feel better. Just glad that the interview was over.

Vic was sitting on the chair outside the police department that she had previously occupied. She was sitting ramrod straight, not slouched over. If she was guilty, she wouldn't be there. She would have taken Erin's twenty dollars and found the quickest way she could out of town.

Unless she knew she was being tailed and was waiting for the right opportunity to present itself.

Vic gave her a tired smile. "All done? I feel like I've been up since three o'clock."

"Maybe because you have been."

Vic stood up. She looked a little awkward, as if she didn't know what to do with herself.

"You're coming home with me," Erin said. "We'll both get a good sleep, and…"

"Everything will look better in the morning?"

Erin laughed.

"My mom always used to say that," Vic said apologetically. "I know, it's sort of lame…"

"It's exactly what I was just thinking. It's always been true for me."

Vic sighed and gave Erin a sideways look. "I hope it's true this time."

Erin walked in the front door with a sigh of relief. It was good to be back in the familiar surroundings. It was becoming her sanctum. Starting to feel just a little like home. Vic entered behind her. They were both careful, looking down, watching for the kitten. He might want to run free after being cooped up all day, so they opened the door no farther than they had to in order to slip through the opening, and then shut it quickly behind them.

"Doesn't look like it's been destroyed," Vic observed.

"No. Everything looks fine out here."

She led the way into the house. "Here, kitty, kitty…"

When they went into the kitchen, she heard the skittering of claws and turned to see the orange kitten running toward them. He stopped and sat down, smelling the air. Vic cooed.

"Oh, isn't he just the cutest little thing!" She reached to pick him up. "You aren't big enough to keep someone up at night, are you?"

He tried to avoid her hand, but Vic was too quick and in a minute had the kitten snuggled to her chest and was stroking him and scratching his ears. The kitten started a loud, motorcycle purr.

"Awww…"

"You've got the touch," Erin said. "I couldn't catch him."

"Well, here," Vic handed the kitten to her. "You should hold him, then. Get him used to you."

"He slept on top of my head last night."

Vic giggled. "He's just so precious. I can't believe he's big enough to leave his mama."

"He seems to be able to manage the dry cat food, so that's a good sign. He won't starve and doesn't have to be bottle fed."

Vic patted him with one finger while Erin held him.

"Yeah. That's good."

"Do you want the bathtub first? You probably need it the most."

Vic sniffed at her shirt. "I'm not that bad, am I? I tried to sponge off every day. You know, at the sink. The bathroom one, not the kitchen."

"No, you're not bad at all. I just know it's been a while since you had access to a tub or shower. Do you want it?"

"Yes, yes," Vic said quickly. "I do!"

"Help yourself. Grab a towel from the linen closet at the end of the hall and I'll get you something to change into. I'm shorter than you, so the pants will be too short, but it's just for bed. We'll wash your clothes so that they're fresh for the morning. Do you have other clothes... somewhere?"

"I have a few things stashed," Vic admitted.

"Okay, good. You can bring them back here so that you have what you need for a few days."

Vic stood there looking at Erin.

Erin swallowed and looked away. "What...?"

"Why are you being so nice to me? I mean... my own aunt wouldn't have anything to do with me. You could have told the cops all kinds of things to implicate me and instead you're telling him you don't think I did it. You're a stranger to me."

"That doesn't mean I shouldn't care about you. I think... people should take care of each other."

Vic's eyes glistened. "Maybe you wouldn't say that if you knew more about me."

"I've been where you are... You're right, I don't know your past. But I know what you need."

Vic moved suddenly away from Erin. She left the kitchen and went down the hall to the linen closet. Erin heard her open the bathroom door and turn on the water. Erin looked down at the kitten.

"Okay, then. Vic can have the first bath and I'll get you your dinner. Have you been waiting patiently all day?"

The kitten purred and kneaded Erin with sharp claws. Erin quickly detached him and put him down on the kitchen floor again. The kitten looked up at her towering over him. She must be like a monster to him.

"It's okay," Erin said softly. "Let's get you some food."

She felt bad about only having the hard kibble intended for adult cats and looked through the pantry for something else appropriate. There was no canned cat food, but there was tuna. Erin grabbed it and picked up the cat's dish. As soon as she had the can open, the fishy smell flooded the room and the kitten was rubbing around her ankles, making excited little *mrrrow* noises. He obviously liked what he was smelling. Erin liked a tuna sandwich now and then, but the smell was so strong she had to breathe through her mouth to avoid gagging. Erin started with half the can of tuna and sprinkled in some of the dry kibble. She added a splash of water and stirred it, leaving it on the counter for a minute to soften. She refreshed the water dish, which the kitten sniffed at. He took a couple of laps, as if to show his gratitude, but then went back to trying to climb straight up the cupboards to sink his teeth into the good stuff. At least he wasn't trying to climb her leg.

In a couple more minutes, the kitten was gobbling down his gourmet supper. Erin went to her room to get some clothes for Vic, and then to Clementine's room to prepare it for company. It only took a couple of minutes to change the sheets.

"Clothes for you," Erin announced as she poked her head into the bathroom and put the clothes down on the counter. Vic jumped and instinctively turned away from her. But with the shower curtain pulled shut, Vic's modesty was protected. Erin chuckled. "See you in a few minutes."

"I won't be long," Vic promised, her voice sounding strange in the enclosed space of the bathroom. "I won't use up all the water."

Erin went up to the attic room to read for a few minutes while she waited for Vic to get out. She was finally able to focus on her book, relaxed, but not too sleepy. Or maybe it was just the sound of the shower below her, and having someone else in the house, so it didn't seem so quiet and lonely.

She always told herself that she didn't get lonely. She had lived on her own for so long, how could she? She liked to be independent and have her own space. But her little family had grown from one to three and she liked the feeling of having others around her. Her life felt more... cushioned. Like she

113

was safely in a nest instead of rattling around the empty house, all hard surfaces and sharp edges.

"Erin?"

Erin startled at Vic's voice somewhere close at hand. She had been engrossed in her book and hadn't noticed the shower turning off.

"I'm up here." Erin got up and went to the top of the stairs. Vic was peering up at her. "Come on up."

Vic hesitated. She put her foot on the bottom step. "Are you sure? I thought this might be your... retreat. Maybe you don't want other people in your space?"

"No, come have a look."

Vic ascended the stairs without any more persuasion. She looked around the attic room.

"This is awesome! Really! I love it."

"Me too. Come up here to read, write, or just chill out. No distractions. It's so restful."

"You have the perfect little house. You're so lucky!" Vic covered her mouth and reddened. "Sorry. I mean... it's not lucky when someone dies. That's not the right word."

"It's okay," Erin assured her. "It was a great opportunity for me. I never had anything like this before. I never thought I would. I was just living day to day, trying to make ends meet. Trying to keep myself from going crazy. And then suddenly... I had this. It still hasn't really sunk in. I keep thinking... someone will come and tell me it was all a joke. Or a mistake. That it isn't really mine and I don't have any rights to any of it."

Vic nodded. "Yeah. I can understand that."

Erin stood up and stretched. "But... no point in stressing out over these things. Whatever happens, happens. We have to enjoy what we have right now, because no one knows what we might or might not have tomorrow. It could all be gone in a day."

She went over to the stairs and paused.

"Do you want to stay up here, or do you want me to show you your bedroom?"

"I'm ready for bed. It's been a long day."

"Come on, then. Light switch is here, just hit it before you come down."

Erin waited at the bottom of the stairs, then showed Vic how to fold them back up to the ceiling. Vic stared up at them.

"That's just really cool."

"It is." Erin agreed. She went to Clementine's room and indicated it. "This one is yours. There are fresh sheets on the bed. We'll clear out some closet space after you retrieve your things."

Vic looked at the room, her mouth falling open. "But... this is the master bedroom, isn't it? This is your room."

"I'm in the next one down. I wasn't comfortable with this one. So, you'll have to deal with it. This was my aunt's room. I don't think I could sleep in here, thinking about her. But you didn't know her. You should be fine."

"You don't want this one?"

"Nope."

"Well... you'll let me know if you change your mind? Because it's your room. You should be able to sleep in your own room."

"I'll let you know if I change my mind. But that's not going to happen in the near future."

Vic tiptoed into the room. Erin giggled at the sweat pants which climbed almost to her knees. Vic looked down at her legs and shook her head. "You're right about them being too short. But they're fine for sleep."

"Good. I'll say goodnight now and see you in the morning. We'll need to be up bright and early."

"That's the plan. Thanks so much, for everything. You've done more than anyone could be expected to."

Erin patted her on the arm and headed back to the bathroom. There was a moment of silence, and then Vic closed her bedroom door.

Chapter Ten

ERIN WOKE UP IN the morning with the kitten sleeping on the pillow against her cheek. Erin's nose tickled and she sneezed, making the kitten jump up and stare at her indignantly. Erin laughed.

"Serves you right for sleeping against my nose! I can't help it, you know. You got your fluff up my nasal passages!" She sneezed again and the kitten jumped down from the bed. He made a little noise as he exited the room.

After getting dressed, Erin pulled Vic's clothes out of the dryer and knocked on the door.

"Got your clothes."

She just about walked into the door when the knob didn't turn in her hand. It was locked. Erin stared at the door for a moment, surprised, then knocked again.

"Vic? It's time to get up, Vic. Rise and shine! I'll leave your clothes here outside the door."

There was a groan from within, which Erin took as acknowledgment. She went into the kitchen to feed the kitten and have a quick bite to eat before heading to the bakery. And coffee. She needed coffee.

Mrrrow, mrrrow! The kitten rubbed against her legs, making excited noises.

"Yes, you can have the rest of the tuna this morning. Just wait a minute while I get it ready for you."

The cat continued to chirrup and patted at the cupboards, trying to climb up to where Erin was working. Erin did not enjoy the smell of tuna first thing in the morning.

Erin heard Vic open her door and head across the hall to the commode. In a few more minutes, she was in the kitchen, sniffing at the air like the cat.

"Coffee?"

"Over there," Erin indicated the machine. "Grab a to-go cup, because we need to be on our way soon." Erin bent down to put down the cat's dish. "I'm going to put some fresh papers down in the bathroom, just in case. Do you need anything else?"

Vic shook her head. "No, I think I'm good."

"There are bagels. Or—"

"I'm not the kind of person who can eat first thing in the morning. I'll have something at the bakery later, once my stomach wakes up."

"Okay." Erin nodded. "No problem."

She went to the back door where the newspapers and other recycling were stored. She took the top newspaper from the pile. It was a few months old. Erin picked it up and glanced over the headlines.

Sleepy little town. Not much happened there.

But under the newspaper was another kind of paper. This one oversize, the paper yellow, brown at the edges, and crumbly. Erin picked it up. She carried it back to the kitchen with the newspaper, studying it.

"Vic, look at this."

"What is it?"

"It's a map."

Vic leaned over her shoulder, looking at it. "A map of what?" She frowned. "That's out on the mountain somewhere? It looks really old."

"Yeah. It does." Erin studied it. "I think it's a mining survey." She glanced at her watch. "We'll have to look at it tonight. Got to get in to the bakery now."

Erin had awoken that day with new resolve. If she wanted to prove her and Vic's innocence, she needed to find other suspects for Officer Piper to focus on.

The question that loomed up before her to begin with was who had a key. Someone had unlocked the back stairway door and probably relocked the back door to the parking lot. She just needed to find out who had keys.

"How's your new little assistant working out?" Mary Lou asked, putting down her tall coffee cup to pay for her muffin. She straightened her blouse and smiled in Vic's direction.

"Vic is really a help. I don't know how I thought I was going to run the place by myself. I could even use a third person, someone in the kitchen, to keep things running and make sure we don't let something burn in the oven."

Erin was keeping her ears open for the timer, but was afraid that she would miss it with the conversation and the noise of the till. She really should bring her timer to the front to keep an eye on it instead of leaving it in the back. That would make a lot more sense.

"It's a lot of fun," Vic said.

"I'm glad you think so." Erin didn't hand Mary Lou her money right away. "Mary Lou... you knew my Aunt Clementine, didn't you?"

"Everyone knew Clementine, dear. Well, maybe not so much the last few years, with her being mostly housebound and new people moving into town, but before that, when she was running the tea room, everybody knew who she was."

"Yes, but I'm wondering who was particular friends with her."

Mary Lou held her hand out for her change and Erin handed it over. "Well, Clementine was very well-liked. She had a smile and a kind word for everyone. Like you and Vic. Unlike some recently deceased who went around sour-pussed all the time, acting like the world owed her something."

"I thought you were friends with Angela."

"As close as anyone. Which is to say, not very close at all. We were on speaking terms. Of course we would talk, exchange pleasantries. But Angela wasn't an easy person to know. She was angry and pushed people away. She got people involved in... questionable business dealings. She was... self-righteous and closed-minded..." Mary Lou gave a sweet smile. "Not to speak ill of the dead."

"No... I didn't realize. I thought she was just like that toward me, because of the bakery. I thought you were all friends. You didn't think I should start a bakery either. Why would you be loyal to Angela's bakery if you didn't like her?"

"My loyalty does not require that I like her, my dear."

Erin realized she had let herself get diverted from her initial question and there were other customers waiting while she talked with Mary Lou. "I was just wondering about Clementine. About who she was friends with. I'm... trying to find a key."

"A key?" Mary Lou looked mystified. She stepped aside so that Erin could run the next couple of customers' orders through the till, but stayed close enough to talk. "What key are you looking for?"

Erin hadn't prepared a lie. Which, of course, she should have done, since she couldn't tell the holders of the store keys that they were suspects in the murder investigation. She deliberately ran into difficulty with the next couple of orders, trying to come up with a good explanation for Mary Lou.

"There's a locked cabinet in the storeroom downstairs," she explained, dropping her voice confidentially and leaning toward Mary Lou. "I didn't really think anything of it before, but this morning Vic and I found an old map hidden at Clementine's house. A really old map. Civil War era, maybe. It wasn't until then that I remembered Clementine told me years ago, when I was just a little girl, that there was a secret in the old cabinet. A clue to find a treasure. So, now I'm wondering," Erin cut her eyes left and right as if to make sure no one but Mary Lou was listening, "if it's something to do with this map."

Mary Lou's eyes were wide. "But why would someone else have the key to Clementine's locked cabinet? What happened to her key?"

There was a lull in the line of customers while a young lady in a suit looked over the goods, trying to make a decision.

"I thought maybe she gave the key to the cabinet to someone with the spare key to the store. Maybe she got her key chains mixed up and gave the one with the cabinet to someone to hold on to when she closed up the store. She might not have even remembered about the cabinet, after she got frail…"

"How fascinating. But I don't remember Clementine ever mentioning anything like that. About a treasure or a map."

"She said it was a family secret. I don't know, maybe it was ill-gotten gains from some ancestor. You know how some of those Civil War villains were…"

"Every family has got some bad ones," Mary Lou agreed.

"And you heard about my ghost, didn't you?"

"Melissa did mention something about that! But this shop has never had a ghost before. I would have known. Clementine would have told us." Mary Lou shook her head slightly.

"Maybe the ghost is Clementine. That's what Officer Piper thought. Or maybe Clementine or I somehow disrupted a ghost that hadn't been active before." Erin tried to remember what Melissa had suggested. She hoped she didn't sound too flippant. How would she talk if she believed in ghosts? "Maybe someone… disturbed it."

"By taking the map home?" Mary Lou suggested. "Maybe it was the map that was in the cabinet. Are you sure there is still something in there? I can't imagine her closing up the shop and leaving something that was potentially valuable behind."

"Maybe," Erin agreed. "But why lock the cabinet again if it was empty?"

Mary Lou withdrew slowly, turning toward the door. "Well, you just let me think on it. I'll see what I can come up with."

"Do you really think that map is to a buried treasure?" Vic asked when they closed up to have their lunches. Obviously, she had heard at least part of Erin's conversation with Mary Lou.

"No, of course not. Why would she put a treasure map in the recycling? It wasn't something valuable to her. I just thought... I needed an excuse to be asking around for keys to the bakery. And I already had the map on my mind, I guess, so I just concocted a story around that."

"Oh." Vic nodded. Erin wondered if she detected disappointment in the girl's expression.

"Sorry. Were you all ready to go hunting treasure?"

"Yeah, kinda. It sounds like fun."

"Well, according to that map, there are all kinds of caves and mines around here. There must be a few places where a person could go exploring."

"Spelunking."

"What?"

"Exploring caves? It's called spelunking."

Erin gave a shiver. "That makes it sound creepy. I have visions of slimy cave walls and white fish in a pitch-black underground lake."

Vic nodded. "Exactly."

"Ew. I'm not sure I'd be up for that. But we should ask around, there are probably a few caves that a novice could explore without a bunch of expensive equipment... and blind white fish."

"Maybe there are cave paintings. I've always wanted to see some real cave paintings."

Erin nodded, chewing her sandwich. Cave paintings would be near the surface. Easily accessible. And they would probably be a really popular place to visit, so there would be guides and lights and railings to prevent people from falling over underground cliffs. Or into underground lakes full of blind, white fish.

"Maybe we could do that some Sunday afternoon, after the church ladies are done their tea."

"We're open on Sunday? Here?"

"Just for the after-church social. Then we can close the doors and go exploring."

"I don't think they'll like that." Vic shook her head slowly, dubious.

"You don't think they'll like what? Us being open after church?"

"Us going cave exploring on a Sunday."

"Why would they care about that?"

"Because of the Sabbath," Vic pointed out. "They don't like people doing... secular stuff on Sunday."

"But it wouldn't have anything to do with them."

Vic continued to shake her head. Erin studied her.

"Do you believe in God?" she asked. "And the Sabbath and all that?"

Vic was hesitant. She looked toward the front door, as if hoping someone would stop by and save her from answering the question.

"You don't have to answer," Erin said. "Sorry. That's a really personal thing to ask. I don't care whether you do or don't believe in God. I was just curious. Wondering how you felt about it."

"I believe in God," Vic said. "I just don't know... what kind of God. I don't like the idea of a God that punishes people for... I don't know, breaking the Sabbath or some other commandment. I'm not too sure about Jesus being a god on earth, but I like his ideas about loving people, even the sinners. I've looked a little bit into other religions, Buddhism and so on. But I haven't really made up my mind... what it is I believe. I guess I'm still Christian... for now."

Erin got up to pour herself a glass of milk. She held it up. "You want one?"

"Yeah, sure."

"Were you raised religious? Christian?"

"Yeah. Pretty much. I mean, we didn't really go to church except maybe sometimes at Christmas, which was kind of neat. But my parents taught me right and wrong... from that perspective."

"Meaning they punished you for breaking the rules they cared about?"

"They weren't really bad. I mean, a lot of kids are abused, physically beaten really bad by their parents, or one of them. I wasn't punished like that. It was more... emotional... psychological. And then when I... strayed too far... they kicked me out. But I was old enough to be on my own. It wasn't like I was fourteen or something. I'm an adult..."

She trailed off and Erin wondered how close that was to the truth. It seemed like there was an 'almost' at the end of that sentence.

"You're eighteen?"

"Uh, yeah. So, I'm an adult and it's okay that I'm on my own."

"Except that you didn't have anywhere to go. No job, no home, no prospects. You might be an adult, but you're still pretty young. Pretty tough to be trying to start out all on your own when you're that young."

"I guess. It's been hard. I came here, thinking that Aunt Angela would let me stay with her until I got onto my feet. Maybe even offer me a job at her bakery. I always liked it here."

"I don't understand anyone who turns a kid out on the street. Not your parents, not your Aunt Angela... I just can't understand it. People should help each other. Especially young people."

"I sure appreciate the way you're helping me out," Vic spoke around a mouthful of sandwich. Then, realizing what she had done, she covered her mouth as she finished chewing and swallowing it. "Sorry. I'm going to pay you back for everything you've done for me, as soon as I can. Except I guess it's all going to come out of your pocket, since you're the one paying me. Kind of hard to pay you back for letting me work by giving you back the money you gave me..."

"There's got to be a tax advantage there somewhere. Don't worry about paying me back. People have helped me from time to time... I just want to do the same for someone else."

"You've done more than anyone else, even the people who are supposed to know and love me." She grinned. "And after I broke into your store and smashed your coffee mug."

"The coffee mug I expect you to replace!" Erin said severely, wagging her finger at the girl. Then she giggled. "We'd better open back up. I can see people gathering out there."

"It seems like a strange time for a rush." Vic looked at the clock on the wall. "It shouldn't be the lunch rush yet."

"Maybe everyone is hungry early."

Erin went up to the door, flipped the sign, and unlocked the door. She smiled at Melissa and Gema, but she felt uneasy about them both showing up at once and at such an odd time.

"What can I get for you ladies today?"

They walked up to the display case and alternated between looking at the products and at the board on the wall, neither one in a particular hurry.

"I hear you're trying to find some keys," Gema said casually.

"Yes, I am," Erin agreed. She pointed to the chocolate chip cookies. "I know you're probably just here for an early lunch, but those are fresh out of the oven."

"Oooh... those do look good," Gema admitted. She pushed her hair back behind her ear. "I'll take a dozen."

"Do you want twelve or thirteen?"

Gema raised her brows. "Is there a price point difference? Usually a baker's dozen is just an extra cookie for the same price."

"Same price," Erin confirmed. "But Mary Lou, when she bought some the other day, didn't want thirteen because her family can't split them up evenly."

Gema laughed. "That sounds just like Mary Lou. No, thirteen is fine with me. My husband will eat most of them, but no one keeps track."

Erin started counting them out. "Is it just you and your husband at home, then? I don't really know about anyone's families."

"Yes. Kids are grown and gone, so it's just me and Fred now."

"Empty nesters."

"We're quite happy to have the nest to ourselves, truth be told. No boomerang kids, if we can help it."

Erin nodded. "Boys or girls?"

"Three boys. I always wanted a little girl, but… Fred and I only ever had boys…"

"Maybe you could adopt or foster a girl. An older child."

"I'll bet you didn't go back to your parents after you left the nest." Gema changed the subject abruptly.

"Umm… no. My parents are dead. I didn't have anyone to go back to. Once I hit eighteen, I was on my own. No safety net."

"Oh, my! Well, that's the way the birds do it. And you seem like you turned out okay. A responsible young woman. Owner of your own baking establishment."

Erin handed her the bag of cookies and waited for payment. Gema poked around in her wallet, laying down bills and coins one at a time. Eventually, she had the right amount and pushed it over to Erin.

"Except I didn't exactly earn this place," Erin reminded her. "It was left to me by Clementine. So, I guess... there was a safety net. Eventually. But it took a few years to find it."

"You could very well have just liquidated everything and blown the cash on drugs or an exotic vacation. But you didn't. You started a business. And not Clementine's business," Gema held up a finger. "Your own business. What you wanted to do. No matter what anyone said."

"I guess I'm past needing anyone's approval." Erin turned to Melissa. "And what would you like?"

"Getting back to the keys..."

Erin had been enjoying Gema's and Melissa's looks of frustration as she led the topic away from the treasure hunt.

"The keys?"

"You were looking for a lost key? To something Clementine had?"

"Right. I guess Mary Lou must have told you about it. So far, no one has come forward with any keys. Clementine must have been the only one who had keys to this store. Just the ones I got from the lawyer."

"Clementine had more keys than that," Melissa protested. "Everyone around here has everyone else's keys. I look at the keys on my rack at home and I don't even know which ones belong to who anymore. A lot of good that does!"

"Everyone has everyone else's keys? Why even have keys, then? Why not just leave the door open for whoever comes by?"

"You couldn't do that!" Gema protested, jumping back into the conversation. "We may not have a lot of crime in Bald Eagle Falls, but there are still robberies. Drug addicts who drift through. Things... could still happen. But sharing your keys with your friends, that's just neighborly and good policy."

"So, did you have any of Clementine's keys?" Erin looked from one to the other.

"Why, I'd have to know what I was looking for, like I said," Melissa reminded her. "I wouldn't recognize them myself. Can you describe the key that you're looking for?"

"You don't put tags on the keys? Clementine's Tea Room? Something like that?"

"I guess that would be the smart thing to do. Everybody just hands you whatever they've got on hand. Then you put it on your peg board, or in your junk drawer, and in six months, you can't remember where they came from." She gave a laugh.

"Huh." Erin turned to the next woman in line, a large woman in a red blazer who Erin thought might have been there opening day.

Melissa and Gema waited impatiently while Erin served her.

"You don't know if you had any of her keys?" Erin asked.

"What did this key look like?" Melissa persisted. "This key to a cabinet. How big? What do you think is in the cabinet?"

"How would that help you find the key? It's just a little one, I guess. Half the size of a door key. Probably a little brass key. Old."

"Old? How old?"

"I don't know. The cabinet has been there as long as I can remember. But if Clementine never gave you any keys, there's no point in worrying about it."

"And what do you think is in the cabinet? Mary Lou said something about a treasure map?" Gema asked.

"It's not a treasure map. Just an old map. And I'm sure it's nothing important. Maybe it was just something to do with her genealogy, or a cave she wanted to explore when she had the time." Erin thought she'd better play down the treasure angle. It was just a little too fanciful for anyone to believe. But minimizing it only seemed to encourage the women.

"But the cabinet is locked. Like something was left there. Forgotten, all this time."

"Do you have any of Clementine's keys?" Erin demanded. "There's no point in even talking about it unless you have Clementine's keys."

Gema and Melissa exchanged looks. They weren't, Erin thought, rolling their eyes at her demand, or exchanging a knowing look. Instead, they looked like they were sizing each other up. Weighing what they wanted to say in front of the other.

If they had something to hide, they shouldn't have come in together. Had they just been swept up in the excitement of a mysterious treasure map and hadn't thought of the consequences? Mary Lou had been a lot more wary about buying into the idea of a secret to a treasure hunt.

"I'm sure Clementine did give me keys at one time," Melissa admitted slowly. "But I'll have to look for them. I just thought if you could describe the one you were looking for, it would make it a lot faster."

"Would you mind returning any of Clementine's keys to me? Even if it's not the key to the cabinet, I'm supposed to be inventorying them and getting the locks changed."

It was Gema who narrowed her eyes at this statement. "Why do you need to inventory the keys if you're getting the locks changed?"

"Well... that's what the lawyer told me I needed to do. I guess maybe in case there are keys to other things that we don't know about, like the cabinet. Maybe... a safety deposit box or storage locker somewhere. Or a safe at the house. They weren't sure they had identified all her assets and there could be something else."

"She wouldn't have given anyone her safety deposit key or anything like that. They would be on her own key chain. She would have wanted to keep them safe."

Erin gave a shrug. Maybe she wasn't as good of a liar as she thought she was. Her stories kept unraveling on examination. "That's what the lawyer said. I wouldn't want to get cross-threaded with him."

"I'll have to look through what I've got," Melissa said. She looked at Gema. "You don't think *you* had anything like that, do you?"

"No. I don't know if there ever was a key to that cabinet. I never heard Clementine say anything about it. Maybe it's just a cabinet with a stuck door. Are you sure it's locked? Is it one of those flimsy sheet-iron things? You can generally pop one of those right open with a crowbar."

"I didn't think of that."

Both women looked toward the door that led down to the basement. Each eyed the other.

"Sorry, it's closed," Erin said. "I'm not supposed to let anyone down there until the police have cleared it. You know, in case there's still evidence… some evidence as to who it was that killed Angela."

Gema shook her head. "That's so ridiculous. I can't believe little Terry Piper would go so far as to claim that it was murder. It was obviously just accident. Angela had severe, life-threatening allergies. She got exposed to something. And she died. It wasn't anyone's fault and it certainly wasn't murder. That's ridiculous."

Erin smiled at Gema calling the policeman 'little Terry Piper.' She obviously remembered him from his younger days, before he was the law in Bald Eagle Falls. She imagined Piper trying to give her a ticket and Gema waving her finger at him, telling him that he needed to do more research, or go home and practice his piano, or something from whatever other role she had played in his past. Gema worked at one of the stores in town. Maybe she had caught Piper shoplifting once as a child.

"Well, if either of you can return Clementine's keys to me, and let me know if you can think of anyone else she might have given a key to…"

"I'll look through my keys," Melissa agreed. She turned and looked at the silent Gema. "And what about you, Gema? You have a set of Clementine's keys, don't you?"

"I would have to look. I got rid of a lot of old stuff. I doubt I do anymore."

And if she had used them to commit the murder, she wouldn't be handing them over to Erin any time soon. Anyone who turned keys over to Erin was unlikely to be the murderer. It would be someone who claimed not to have keys.

"What about Mary Lou? Would she have had keys?"

"Didn't you ask her?"

"She didn't say she did. I'm just wondering... I mean. She might have forgotten."

"If anyone had a key, it would be Mary Lou," Gema said. "She was the closest one to Clementine. Her or Angela."

"You think Angela might have had a key?" Erin asked, surprised at Gema's guess. Hadn't Mary Lou said that no one really liked Angela? "Why would she have had one?"

"They were friendly. Clementine made a little bit of baking, but mostly she bought from Angela. They were probably back and forth to each other's shops all the time. It would make sense for them to have a way to get in and out. Angela would be up before the birds to bake bread and she could put it in Clementine's shop before opening up her own store. Or if Clementine ran out of something, she could run over and get it, and they would settle up over it later."

Erin avoided looking at Vic. She was sure Vic was straining her ears to hear every word she could. Funny how their lives were mirrors of each other. Their aunts friends together, running their businesses with each other. The aunts both eventually dying, and now their nieces, side by side, trying to unravel the threads of what had happened before Clementine shut down her business. Before Angela was murdered.

Was the secret to the murder in the recent past? Or years ago? Was one of the three ladies responsible for what had happened to her? Or did they know something that would identify the killer? The threads of their lives had obviously all been intertwined.

Before she could think of anything else to ask, both women were saying goodbye and heading out the door. Erin watched them go and sighed, turning to look at Vic.

Vic gave a little shrug and they continued to work together without comment until the lunch rush was over and the shop was empty again for a few minutes. Erin put some more muffins in the oven for the after-school crowd. Kids and teachers looking for something sweet at the end of the day. Parents wanting dessert to go with supper or breakfast for their children the next day. She was starting to get a feeling for the ebb and flow of the people going through the shop.

Erin was rearranging the products in the display case when she saw a man walk by the big window. At first, she saw just a dark and threatening shadow, then realized she had seen him somewhere before. But where? She hadn't been to that many places in town. He could have been working or shopping at one of the stores she had been to.

But even through the window, he seemed grimy and work worn. Not like someone who worked in a shop or at a desk. Someone who belonged on an oil rig or down a mineshaft. Maybe a welder.

"What...?" Vic followed her gaze.

"That man out there. Do you know him?" It was probably silly to ask Vic. Vic had been there a little longer than Erin, but she had been hiding out, not out meeting people.

"Uh, yeah. William something. Willie... William... is it Anthony? Something like that. William Anthony. No. Andrews. William Andrews." Vic nodded, sure she had hit on it. "Yes. William Andrews."

"How do you know him? What exactly does he do?"

"Drifter. Lazy good-for-nothing," Vic said. When Erin looked at her in astonishment, open-mouthed, Vic grinned. "Aunt Angela's words, not mine. I don't think he's a lazy good-for-nothing. I've always seen him working. Odd jobs. Maybe that's why Aunt Angela thought he was lazy. Because he didn't have one steady job. But he's always doing something. Not begging or living off of anyone else."

"How do you know that? I thought your aunt wouldn't let you stay around. It didn't sound like you sat down to discuss the pros and cons of each of the town's residents."

"No." Vic laughed. "Other years. I used to come here to do work for Aunt Angela sometimes. Just give her a hand with whatever she needed done around the store. And she talked about people. More than she should."

Erin nodded, accepting this. Though Vic's words niggled at her. If Vic had come to Bald Eagle Falls in past years, why didn't people know her? Everyone seemed to accept that she was a friend of Erin's, an outsider they had never met before.

"So, William Andrews has been around for a few years. He's not someone who just drifted into town recently."

"No. I don't think he's from here originally, so that makes him a drifter as far as Aunt Angela is concerned. Not Bald Eagle Falls prime stock."

"That's a pretty narrow view."

"Aunt Angela had a lot of narrow views. I didn't really understand that until I came back here. She was the aunt who always had something in the cookie jar. And who paid me to do jobs for her. I thought she was a pretty good person. I didn't understand that she... she was really prejudiced against all kinds of people."

"Prejudiced?" Erin's mind had been wandering and the word drew her back. "What kind of people was she prejudiced against?"

That was just the type of insider information Erin needed. Anyone Angela was prejudiced against would be a prime suspect. She had been unfair to them, they had retaliated...

"Everyone," Vic said. "I didn't realize how she found fault with everyone. It wasn't just the people who didn't follow the rules of her house. William Andrews was a drifter, because he wasn't born here. He was a good-for-nothing because he didn't have one job. She always had something to say about Blacks or immigrants. People who weren't educated, or who were too educated and thought they were better than she was. People who wouldn't get involved in investments or another one of her schemes, they were scared rabbits. Gutless. But the people who did get involved and complained about her losing their money were just whiners. Worthless, no-account people who didn't know what they were talking about or how risky the market was." Vic shrugged. She shook her head, as if reliving a private hurt that she couldn't tell Erin about. Something worse. Erin wondered what it was.

"Did she say who had invested and lost money?"

"I don't know. I suppose. But I kind of got the feeling that it was everyone, at one time or another. She acted like the whole town was against her."

"And yet, she wouldn't take in one person who wasn't against her," Erin observed.

Vic turned her back to take some dishes to the sink, sliding them carefully into the soapy water.

"What kind of odd jobs does William Andrews do?" Erin asked, when Vic returned to the front of the shop.

"I'm not sure. He drives things around. Like a courier or hot shot service. He does yard work. Painting. Cleaning. Lots of different things."

Then Erin remembered where she knew him from. He had been the man who had helped her—or tried to help her—to unload groceries when she was first stocking up the bakery. She'd had to chase him off, because he was being so persistent and making her uncomfortable. Maybe he had just wanted to help. Maybe he had expected a couple of dollars by way of tip for having helped her out. If the poor man was destitute, surviving on odd jobs, maybe it had been wrong of her to chase him away like that. He had said that he only wanted to help.

"Oh, yeah," she said. "I remember him."

Had Andrews known who Erin was and what she was doing, opening up the specialty bakery? He had been the one person who had gotten close to her flours and other baking supplies. Was it possible he had tampered with something? If Angela had bullied him for not having a job, maybe he had decided to take his revenge. And the missing autoinjector was just a coincidence. The icing on the cake. Or maybe he had done a job for her and picked her pocket.

"Was he here on opening day?"

"I don't know," Vic reminded her. "I wasn't around on opening day."

"Oh, that's right. I'm sure I would have noticed him." Erin remembered how busy opening day had been. "Maybe. But not if he had a key and came through the back. If he did odd jobs for Clementine, maybe he had a key. It doesn't seem like he could have contaminated one of the ingredients… No one else reported reacting to any of the baking. It seems like Angela was the only one. Like it was targeted."

Vic raised an eyebrow, listening with interest to Erin rambling on. "So, is he another suspect?"

"Maybe. But it is a reach. I'll have to mention him to Officer Piper."

She watched him out the window for a minute. He was putting flyers on cars. Was he being paid by someone else, or trying to drum up for business for himself? He was younger than she remembered from that night. Older than she was, but not by so much. Not a grizzled old man. Handsome, in a way, if it hadn't been for the dirt that seemed to be ingrained in his skin.

Vic caught her staring at the man and raised her brows.

Chapter Eleven

SOMEHOW, WORD THAT ERIN had gotten her hands on a Civil War era treasure map seemed to have spread through the town like wildfire. Bald Eagle Falls might have only had a weekly newspaper, but news obviously traveled much faster through other means. Everyone seemed to have something to say about it, even Peter's mother, when she stopped in to pick up some bread and some cookies. Erin reminded herself that she had been planning to start up a kids' club. She just needed to sit down at the computer and design some kind of membership and point-tracking card. In the meantime, she offered the Foster children each a free cookie.

"I've heard there's all kinds of treasure in the hills," Mrs. Foster said. "Gold for soldiers' payrolls, or valuables stashed away by rich families who didn't want to be pillaged. Some of the rumors go back even further than that. To pirate gold or valuables the early settlers hid from the natives. Or sacred artifacts that natives hid from the settlers!"

"Pirate gold?" Vic echoed. "In Bald Eagle Falls?"

"Pirates!" Peter exclaimed, brandishing an imaginary sword while he munched on a cookie in the other hand. "We should search for pirate gold!"

"No, not right in Bald Eagle Falls," Mrs. Foster said. "In the hills. Hidden in caves. The map Erin found, it's a map of the caves, isn't it?"

Erin smiled as she rang up the bill. "I really don't know how much the map would help anyone searching for treasure.

It is old, but I don't think any of the information is secret. It's just a mining survey or something, not a pirate's map."

"No one knows where all the caves are around here. There are all kinds of stories about lost caves and mines. The hills are riddled with them. Like Swiss cheese."

"Can we search for gold?" one of Peter's sisters begged. "Can we go to a cave?"

"We're not going to a cave," Mrs. Foster told her. "That's all I need. My children getting lost in a cave."

"We wouldn't get lost!" Peter objected.

"Yes, you would. You get lost at the grocery store. What would I do? Go home without all of my children?"

"We don't get lost," Peter said. "Just separated. That's different. We could find our way home."

"From the grocery store, maybe. Not from a cave, deep down in the ground."

The littler girl started to cry and Mrs. Foster rolled her eyes. "What's the matter, Juni?"

"I don't want to get lost in a cave in the ground!"

Mrs. Foster pulled her close. "You are not going to get lost in a cave, Juni. No one is going to get lost in a cave."

As they left the store, Juni continued to whine and snivel, while the others made their plans to go searching for pirate gold.

"Pirate gold?" Erin said to Vic, laughing.

"Never get between a southerner and rumors of treasure!"

"You still want to explore caves?"

"I promise I won't get lost!"

It felt good to go home at the end of a busy day, back to the comfort and familiarity of the house, to pat her furry little fuzzball and just relax. It was nice to have someone else there and not just be knocking around by herself through the empty house.

As she sat on the couch and patted the snoozing kitten, Erin reminded herself that she needed to take care of the household chores, too. Kitty kibble crunched under her feet in the kitchen and the litter box needed to be looked after. She should do some grocery shopping so there was some real food in the kitchen and they could have a substantial supper without having to order in.

But she was so tired after her work days that she just didn't have the energy to do much else.

Vic was sitting across from her, poring over the map like she was looking for Blackbeard's treasure. Erin smiled and looked down at the slim weekly paper that she still hadn't finished reading. Her eyelids were heavy and, by the time she finished reading it, the next one would be out. Aside from an article recapping the news of Angela's murder, there were only a few articles, a couple of weekly columns, and several large blocks of advertising. It shouldn't take her a week to read that much.

But she was still so new in town that she read through each of the advertisements carefully to learn all she could about the other businesses in town. What services they offered, what methods they used to attract business, keywords in their advertising copy. She even studied the graphics and pictures they used to figure out what resonated with the readership base. She would need to start advertising as well. Using the wrong picture or words in her ads would be like flushing her hard-earned money down the toilet.

Erin turned the page and closed her eyes for a moment to rest them. She needed to get herself bathed and off to bed, or she was going to be falling asleep on the couch. She didn't want to end up with a crick in her neck for the next week.

"Can we really go to one of these caves on Sunday?" Vic asked.

Erin startled slightly and opened her eyes. Even after telling herself she couldn't go to sleep on the couch, she was dozing instead of reading the weekly.

"Sure, I don't see why not," she said, rubbing her eyes. "We need to do something to relax. We've been working hard.

We should pick up some groceries too. And…" Erin stifled a yawn, but couldn't stop it, and covered the view of her tonsils as best she could. "And I need to do some cleaning and sorting through some of Clementine's things."

"You won't throw anything out, will you?"

"I don't know yet. I don't know what there is. I certainly don't need to keep all her clothes. And I don't think you want them, do you?"

"She wasn't exactly my size," Vic admitted. Clementine had been a tiny woman. Her pants would be as short on Erin as Erin's were on Vic. "But there are some things that might work okay. Scarves and accessories. You might be able to wear some of her shirts or blazers."

"I don't think so. But I'll see if there's anything either of us wants to keep before I give them away. We're both going to need closet space. We can't just keep living out of boxes and bags."

Vic nodded. "I suppose."

"Just let me know if you want something. I don't mind."

"It's really nice of you letting me live here—"

"Don't start that again. I need you. I had no idea how much I was going to need someone else to help me run the bakery. Even now… I think we could still use another person. What do you think?"

"Maybe," Vic agreed slowly, "but I don't like the idea of having someone else in our space."

Funny how quickly Vic had adopted it as her space.

"We'll work it out. I don't have anyone to hire right away anyway, just thinking about what we're going to need if we're going to stay afloat. If we both run ourselves into the ground, we won't be doing ourselves any favors."

"Yeah."

The kitten stretched and readjusted itself in Erin's lap. He needed a name. She scanned for name ideas on the newspaper page. James? Terrence? The General? She blinked drowsily.

"I think I found the one I want to go to," Vic said.

Erin opened her eyes again. She was going to have to get up; if she sat on the couch any longer, she was going to be asleep for sure. She looked down at the newspaper and saw Vic's picture.

Erin frowned. She rubbed her eyes and looked at the photograph again. It wasn't Vic. It was a boy. A teenager, around Vic's age, but a boy, not a girl. There were similarities between their features. If Angela were Vic's aunt, then maybe she had cousins around as well. Erin studied the words around the photo. A missing boy, several towns away. James. Erin stared at his eyes, fringed with long lashes that would have been the envy of any girl.

She had seen those eyes before and she knew where.

"Vic...?"

Vic looked up from the map, her excited smile fading as she took in Erin's expression. She got up and went to see what Erin was looking at in the paper. Her face lost the pink flush in her cheeks.

"Oh."

"Vic, is this... your twin?"

Vic scratched the back of her neck. "Uh... no."

Erin looked again at the name of the boy. The full name. James Victor Jackson. Vic. "Then... is this you?"

Vic sighed. "Yeah."

Erin tried to process it. To make sense of what was going on. "Did you... dress as a girl so that no one would find you?"

"No." Vic sat down and Erin could see that she was shaking. "I'm sorry. I'll leave if you want me to. I know you probably don't want... someone like me staying in your house."

"Explain it to me. I'm confused."

"I am a girl," Vic asserted. "But... I'm transgender. I was raised as a boy, but my gender identity is female."

"And that's why your parents kicked you out."

"Yes."

"And that's why Angela wouldn't have anything to do with you when you went to her for help."

"She was always nice to me when I presented as a boy. I did work for her during summers and school breaks. Helped around the bakery or her yard or whatever she needed done. She was always really good, paid me, looked after me while I was staying with her. I just thought... that was the logical place to go."

"But when you went to her as a girl, that all changed."

"I've been called names before. I always stood out, even trying my best to be masculine. But Aunt Angela... she was so cruel!" Vic's voice broke. She wiped at her eyes, trying to keep the tears at bay. "And then I didn't know where to go. I didn't know what to do. I knew where she kept the key to Clementine's and I thought I would just stay there a night or two, while I figured out what to do."

Erin was no longer sleepy. She put her arm around Vic's shoulders and gave her a squeeze. Then she rubbed the girl's back.

"I'm so sorry your aunt treated you that way. And your parents. That's not right. Even if they don't agree with your... gender identity... that's not what they should have done. They should have... shown you love and support."

"It goes totally against the way I was raised." Vic sniffled and tried to stop the tears. "I get that. I was raised that there are only two sexes, male and female, and that's it, and whatever parts you're born with, that's what you're stuck as. That God decides, and that's what he makes you, and it's a sin to feel different. So, I get it... they think it's breaking a commandment, just like stealing or murder... But..." her voice broke.

"I know." Erin gave Vic another squeeze. "It's okay."

The kitten was disturbed and got up, climbing from Erin's lap to Vic's.

"Oh! Ow, he's got claws!" Vic picked the kitten up, detaching him carefully from her pants. She held him to her chest to stroke him, bowing her head close to him. He wriggled around, getting fur up her nose. When Vic sneezed, the kitten jumped away, landing on the floor and looking at the two of them as if offended.

Erin laughed. The kitten stalked away. He disappeared into the kitchen.

"We need a name for him," Erin said, wiping the corners of her own eyes. "I mean, kitty is fine, but he should have a name."

Vic got a couple of tissues from a box in a crocheted cover on one of the side tables. She blew her nose. "I have a name for him."

Erin smiled. "What's your idea?"

"Well, he's orange."

"Yes."

"I thought… Orange Blossom."

Erin raised her brows. "Orange Blossom? Kind of a funny name for a cat, don't you think? Especially for a boy cat?"

"People name their cats all kinds of things. And as far as it being too feminine… don't forget who you're talking to."

That made Erin laugh in surprise. "Well, okay, consider the source," she agreed. "I don't know. I'll think about it. We'll see if it sticks, shall we?"

"Okay," Vic agreed.

"And now, I think it's time to get ready for bed. I was falling asleep sitting here reading the paper."

Vic nodded her agreement. Erin got up and headed toward the bathroom.

"Erin…?"

"Yes?"

"You won't tell anyone, will you?"

"That you picked the cat's name? I'm not taking the blame if people think it's weird."

Vic giggled. "No… about me. People here, they're not very open-minded."

"You might find that more people are accepting of you than you think." At Vic's stricken look, she continued. "But I won't out you to anyone. It's up to you to tell people or not. You're really lucky that no one else has matched that picture up with you."

"I know... but if they do, I'll just say he's my twin, or something. Like you thought."

"Okay. That's up to you. Won't folks around here remember you, though? And that you didn't have a twin, when you used to come work for your aunt?"

"I'll just say... we were raised by different parents, or something. Like in that Disney show where the identical twins were raised apart."

"Whatever you want. It's your choice."

Vic let out her breath. "Thanks. And what about... the policeman? Officer Piper. You won't tell him?"

Erin considered that, closing her eyes to focus on the question and imagine the scenarios in which she might have to tell Officer Piper about Vic's situation.

"If he asked me directly, I'm not going to lie to him," she said. "That might get me in deeper water than I'm already in as a murder suspect. And get you in deeper trouble too, if he figures you have something to hide."

"You can't tell him."

"If he asks me something... that leads to me having to tell him about you or else lie, then I will ask him to talk to you about it. That's the most I can do. Let you decide what you want to say. But if I tell him to talk to you about it... you're going to have to tell him."

"Yeah, I know. But you won't bring it up?"

"No. Why would I?"

"Because you would be a lot better off if he put me in jail. We're his two best suspects, so it's better for you if he picks me."

"I'm not throwing you to the wolves, Vic." Erin held Vic's gaze. "I'm not that kind of person. I'm not going to do that to you."

"Okay." Vic breathed out. "You're crazy not to. But okay."

Morning came too quickly. Erin and Vic were at the bakery before dawn to get the day's baking done and rearrange the products in the display case. Erin discovered that Vic had beautiful penmanship and had her write up the labels and the changes to the chalk board.

Officer Piper showed up partway through the morning, after the rush when things had quieted down. He had a cup of coffee and K9 stood alertly at his side, nose quivering as he took in all the scents of the bakery.

"What can I get for you today?" Erin asked, as if he were in there every day and it wasn't startling or worrisome for him to just show up out of the blue.

"Well… what's good? What would you recommend?"

"It's all good. Some people are worried that it's going to taste really weird, have a bad texture or an aftertaste. But it doesn't. It's all pretty much like you would expect baking made with wheat flour to taste like."

Piper nodded, but looked doubtful.

"I've heard that gluten can be bad for some dogs," Erin offered. "Maybe I should carry a few doggie biscuits too. Do you think K9 would like that?"

The dog looked at her, ears pricking up at his name.

"Are you trying to bribe an officer of the law?" Piper asked, his face and voice serious. But she could see by the beginnings of the dimple in his cheek and the sparkle in his eye that he was teasing.

"No, I would never do that!" Erin declared, drawing out her vowels and forcing her eyes wide open. Then she fluttered her lashes at him.

She became aware that her heart was racing. Not because she was anxious about him showing up there, but because she was enjoying the attention of the handsome officer. Disconcerted, she looked over the display case to see what product she should be trying to move. But even looking away from him, she was still aware of him. The scent of his aftershave tickled her nose.

"Let's see, the chocolate chip zucchini loaf is a hot seller," she said, even though it wasn't, and that was why she wanted to sell it to him. "Or if you prefer a savory bread for sandwiches or to be paired with soup, this jalapeño cheese bread is just to die for!" She covered her mouth, realizing what she had said. "I mean… it's really good. If you like a little bit of a kick. Do you like things… uh… spicy?"

She could feel rather than hear Vic laughing beside her. Erin's face got hot as she grew more flustered. Piper just stood there looking at her, the corner of his mouth twitching.

"So, chocolate chip zucchini bread, or jalapeño cheese bread?" she asked briskly.

"Well, I do like spicy…" Piper trailed off, considering. His eyes twinkled. "But I also like sweet."

Erin used the tongs to grab a slice of the zucchini bread and put it into a paper snack bag. Then she selected a small loaf of the jalapeño cheese bread and put it into a longer sleeve.

"Something for now, and something for later," she announced. "If you don't use the cheese bread tonight, wrap it in plastic to keep it from drying out too much. Then just warm it in the oven for a few minutes before eating to crisp it up a bit." Erin watched Vic ring it up on the register and complete the transaction with Officer Piper.

"Be sure to come back in a couple of days," Erin told him. "I'll be sure to have some biscuits ready for K9."

Piper nodded. "I'll be back," he agreed.

And he walked back out without a single question about the murder.

"You and the cop?" Vic demanded, after the door had closed behind Officer Piper. "Holy cow! And you the prime murder suspect? Or one of them?"

"I don't know what you're talking about," Erin said. "I just sold the man a few baked goods."

Vic flapped her hand at her throat, fanning herself. "Is it hot in here, or is it just you? Just selling him a few baked goods? I don't think so!"

"He paid for them."

"Yeah. He did. And he'll be back for more."

"Well then, that's just good business, isn't it?" Erin said brightly, with an innocent smile.

"He's good for what ails you, all right."

"I don't know what you mean."

Erin ran into Melissa at the grocery store and took the opportunity to chat with her for a few minutes to get her views on Angela Piper and her murder. She wasn't investigating, exactly. Just getting to know one of her clients better. Getting a bit more background on Vic's aunt. Definitely not investigating.

"So, what did you think about Angela?" Erin asked, as they both considered the various yogurts, sour cream, and soft cheeses in the dairy case.

"What did I think of her?" Melissa let the question hang for a few minutes, then gave a little shrug. "I don't know. What am I supposed to think of her? She was a fixture here. The owner of the bakery and all. And now she's dead. I don't know anything about it. Not sure what you're looking for from me."

"Nothing special," Erin said. "I just never really got a chance to know her. And I'm wondering now... what she was like. Were the two of you friends?"

"We were all friendly with each other," Melissa deflected. "Me and Angela, Gema, Mary Lou, other ladies from the church. We all did things together. Worshiped. Had some fun.

145

Gossiped and commiserated. Everybody knew everybody else."

"You knew each other for a long time?"

"Not as long as Gema, maybe. I'm quite a bit younger than either of them. But yeah, we all knew each other. It was nice now and then, to get together to do something."

"Birthdays, weddings, bridge night…"

"Yes. Like that. Just the girls getting together for a little relaxation. Nothing unusual about that."

"So, you would consider Angela a good friend."

"No… a… friend. An acquaintance. Someone familiar."

"Did you… like her…?" Erin asked tentatively. They were up to the beverages aisle and Erin picked up some club soda. She considered the big display of RC cola, remembering how much she had enjoyed it as a girl when she had come to visit Clementine. But she couldn't drink her calories anymore as an adult. She needed to be disciplined and stick to healthy food and drink. An RC might get her engine going in the morning, but in the evening, it would either keep her up all night, or she would crash and wouldn't be able to get up in the morning. Erin walked on by the display with an iron determination. Melissa reached over and grabbed a big bottle, which she put in her cart. Erin eyed it.

"Do you have children?"

"No, I'm just on my own." She caught the direction of Erin's eyes. "It's for bridge night," she said. "I'm not drinking the whole thing. You wouldn't begrudge me one drink of RC, would you?"

"No, of course not. What you eat is your business. I wouldn't want anyone judging me by what I put in my cart." Erin looked down at several pounds of butter, cream cheese, and sour cream.

"Yes, but everyone knows you run the bakery. It's not like you're eating it all by yourself."

"You can't run a bakery without tasting some of the goods," Erin said. Then she remembered Angela. "Well… I couldn't anyway."

Melissa nodded. "It was hard for Angela. Giving up everything she loved. Not just eating, but baking. It really was her calling."

"Is that why she was so angry?"

"When?"

"All the time, from what I could tell. Wasn't she?"

"Mmm…" Melissa considered. "I wouldn't want to speak ill of the dead."

"No, of course not…"

"It wasn't just not being able to eat things or bake anymore. She was… not a nice person before that, either."

Erin looked at her. Melissa's face was flushed. She turned away from Erin, pretending to be studying the prices on the cold cereal. It wasn't like the specials weren't marked with bright red signage.

"Was she mean to you?" Erin asked. "Is that what you're saying?"

"She was mean to everyone. Not just me. Everybody was afraid of her."

"What did she do to you?"

"I didn't say she did anything to me. Just that she was a mean person. To everyone."

"Okay." Erin pushed her cart down the aisle and let silence do its work. People didn't like silence. They tried to fill the vacuum.

"I went to school with Angela's kids," Melissa offered. Her face was getting redder.

"Did you?"

"Do you know what that was like? She was horrible to her kids."

That hadn't been what Erin had been expecting. "Was she? What happened?"

"Can you imagine having a mother like that? Who would intentionally humiliate you in front of your friends? Punish you? Call you out? With no regard for your privacy at all?"

"That must have been pretty tough on them. Were you… good friends?"

"No!" Melissa's eyes widened and she shook her head. "She wouldn't have let them be friends with me anyway. She never thought anyone was good enough for them, even though she acted like they were worthless. Why do you think none of her kids live in Bald Eagle Falls anymore? They all got out as soon as they could."

"That's pretty sad. Is she married, then? I never heard anyone mention her husband…?"

"No, there hasn't been a man around for a long time."

"Did they divorce or separate? Or did he die?"

"I don't know."

Erin frowned. "How could you not know? I thought everyone knew everyone's business in a town like this."

"She made it this big mystery. She would refer to him all the time, try to intimidate people. 'When I got rid of my husband…' It was actually really creepy."

"So, she… implied that she killed him? Or ran him off?" Erin shook her head. "Or what?"

"That's just it. She never said. Just let everyone draw their own conclusions and wonder what had happened. I expect that he just left her one day. Got tired of all the nagging and complaining and berating him in front of his own children and ran away. I would have, if I'd been living in that house."

"Someone must know."

"I don't know. It's a small town, but when someone just up and disappears without a trace… I'm telling you. No one knows what happened."

"What did the kids say? You said you went to school with them."

"They didn't know. She just told them he was gone and he wasn't coming back."

"And his work? His boss and his coworkers would have reported him missing, wouldn't they?"

"Angela and he worked together. Family business. It started out as his inheritance. The store. The business. But she squeezed him out... until there wasn't anything left of him, financially or physically."

Erin stopped walking and just looked at Melissa. "The business? The bakery was *his* business?"

"Initially, yes. But she just sort of... took over."

"And nobody looked for him when he disappeared?"

"He didn't disappear. Well, he did, but nobody reported him missing. That was up to Angela. She said he wasn't missing, so what was anyone else to do?"

"That's just bizarre."

"That's Angela."

"And the kids, they didn't try to track him down after they left home?"

Melissa added a couple of 'slim' soups to her basket. "The kids are all train wrecks. Davis is an addict. In Seattle, last I heard. Sophie committed suicide. I don't know what happened to Trenton. Like his dad, he just... walked out of Bald Eagle Falls one day and was never heard from again."

"Walked out of Bald Eagle Falls?" Erin repeated. "How could anyone walk out of Bald Eagle Falls? It's in the middle of nowhere."

"He didn't take a car. Didn't get on the bus. Must have walked out and hitched a ride. There was no sign of what had happened to him."

"Two disappearances? And nobody thought anything of it?"

"Trenton *was* reported missing. But the police never turned up a trail. I don't think they tried all that hard. They just figured that he'd gone off like his dad. Turned tail and ran."

"Those poor kids," Erin said, shaking her head. "What a toxic place that must have been."

"I hated that whole family," Melissa said vehemently. Her coy 'I would never speak ill of the dead' manner was gone. The emotion she radiated was raw, almost palpable. Erin saw one of the clerks looking nervously in Melissa's direction. Erin was sure she couldn't have actually heard what Melissa was saying. She could just see or feel the anger and outrage Melissa was giving off. "The whole flippin' family. They were sickos raised by a sicko. Or a psycho. Everyone pussyfooted around here, pretending that Angela was a pillar of the community. She wasn't any pillar, they were just afraid of setting her off. Afraid of what she would do to them if they ever crossed her. They were the most dysfunctional family you ever saw, putting on masks and pretending that they were perfectly normal."

"Did they bully you?" Erin guessed. The anger had to be coming from somewhere. It had to stem from something. Not just a dysfunctional family in the community, but one that had done her wrong. One that had done something that hurt her so badly she couldn't forgive it decades later. It was still an angry, raw wound.

"That Trenton was in my grade. It was a small school, we only had one class per grade. He was always in my class. I could never get away from him. He was always so smarmy and respectful in front of the teacher, they all loved him and thought he was the greatest thing on earth. But when their backs were turned… it was hell. He wasn't an angel; he was a demon. I was glad when he was gone. Glad that he disappeared and never showed his face here again."

"How long ago was that? Did he disappear while you were still in school?"

"He was eighteen. Just barely. Hadn't graduated yet, but was on track to be the class valedictorian or prom king. Or both. He was so smart and the teachers all thought he was so wonderful."

"Then it must have been really strange for him to disappear so suddenly."

"The whole town wanted to know what had happened to him. All the adults, anyway. Not the kids. We were just glad he was gone."

"Do you think..." Erin's mind was racing, trying to make sense of all of the new information. "Do you think that he just took off, ran away, or do you think... someone did something to him? If all the kids hated him so much, do you think there was foul play?"

"I don't know. No one ever said who it was. No one spilled it. If someone did something, they kept quiet about it. Never bragged about it."

"And his family? How did Angela and his siblings react?"

"Just like with his dad. After the initial investigation, they never talked about it again. Angela acted like he hadn't even existed. No pictures up. Never talked about how he had done so well at school or anything like that. She didn't talk about him at all, positive or negative. Just wiped him out."

"Everybody mourns differently," Erin allowed, feeling like she should say something to defend Angela. Surely the woman couldn't have lost her son without feeling something, as Melissa implied. One woman sets up a shrine to her child, and another, unable to bear thinking of him or referring to him again, wipes out everything that would remind her of him.

Melissa just looked at Erin. Erin forced herself to push on, getting some freezer meals so that she and Vic would have something that wouldn't take any energy at the end of a long day. Frozen dinners weren't a great choice, but they would be better than takeout or just eating nothing because no one had the energy to cook.

"So, if Angela was so difficult to get along with," she circled back to the initial topic. "Then there must be a lot of people who were bitter about her."

"A lot of people who wanted to kill her, you mean?"

"Well..." Erin couldn't think of a tactful way to put it. "I suppose, yes. Do you think there were a lot of people who would have wanted to harm her?"

"I don't think anyone was too broken up about it."

"Do the police know all of this stuff about her past? Are they looking into any connections?"

"Officer Piper was younger than us. He would have heard about it when Trenton disappeared. I would guess those old files are around somewhere. Unless they were part of the batch of files we had to destroy that had that dangerous black mold on it. I don't know if Trenton's missing persons file would have been in that batch."

"But he knows about it. Piper. He must be considering any suspects in Trenton's disappearance."

"I guess." Melissa's shoulders rose and fell like it made no difference to her. And maybe it didn't. Maybe she didn't realize that having a key to the shop and being there around the time that Angela was killed made her a suspect. Maybe she didn't think Piper was looking at her and would be looking for any connections to Trenton's disappearance. Like the fact that they had been in the same class at school at the time that Trenton had disappeared. And that she had been one of Trenton's victims.

Had Melissa harbored bitter feelings toward Angela for all those years? Pretending to be friendly with her, playing bridge with her and going to church with her, all the while believing that Angela had made her sadistic son what he was and had been the ultimate cause of Melissa's pain?

Erin gave a shiver, even though they were well past the freezers.

Chapter Twelve

RIN SAT IN HER car for a few minutes in the parking lot of the grocery store, scribbling down lists. She didn't want to forget any of the details of what Melissa had said. If any of it was motive for Angela's murder, she wanted to make sure she had it all down.

After she had recorded everything she could think of, she glanced at the back of the car where the groceries were stacked. She had both groceries needed for the bakery and groceries to be taken home. She knew that she should go back to the shop and put all of her supplies there before going home. She wouldn't want to go out again once she was home. But maybe she could save herself time by just taking everything home with her and then taking it in to the bakery with her the next morning. Instead of having to go two separate places.

But she knew from the start that was a bad idea. That would mean putting things in the fridge at the house and then getting them back out to take with her to the bakery. It meant putting things away twice, which was a waste of time. And she really needed to be efficient with her time.

With a sigh, Erin pulled out and headed over to the bakery. Just a few minutes there to get everything put away, then she could go home and relax. And put away the groceries. And warm up something for supper. And she should do a little cleaning, so that it wouldn't all be piled up for her to do on Sunday after she and Vic got back from their exploring.

She pulled into her parking space behind the store, grabbed a couple of the bags of groceries earmarked for the bakery and hurried to the back door. If she were quick, it wouldn't take so much energy. She had already taken too long at the grocery shopping, listening to Melissa's recollections.

Erin opened the back door and shouldered her way through it before realizing that she had not unlocked it. She knew she had locked it before dropping Vic at home and going grocery shopping. She locked it every day. And Vic would have noticed and reminded her if she had somehow forgotten.

Erin stood just inside the back entrance, holding the groceries, trying to decide what to do.

"Hello? Anybody here?"

She knew that they had keys. The other murder suspects had keys to the shop. She had put in a work order to have the locks on the shop changed out, but the locksmith was apparently on a fishing vacation and could not be talked into coming back to do an emergency job. If she were that desperate, she could get a locksmith from the city. But none of the locksmiths from the city were willing to make the trip out. It wasn't even the money, they just didn't want to make the trip.

So, the shop sat there without the locks being changed. For at least another week.

She thought she heard a noise in the distance. The clink of a tool. Outside? Downstairs?

"Is there somebody here?" Erin called down the stairs.

Was she really expecting someone to answer her? A silly excuse, 'oh, I was just here because I thought I left something incriminating in the bathroom when I murdered Angela.' Or, 'I just wanted a look at that locked cabinet,' or, 'I was just testing to see if these were the keys you were looking for.'

But there was no answer. Erin put down her groceries. She couldn't take them down to the storeroom if there were someone else in the store. Unless…

"Vic, is that you?" Maybe Vic had forgotten one of her possessions there and had walked back over from the house. She might have had something stashed away. Or had left her favorite lipstick in the bathroom by accident.

But there was no reply from Vic.

Erin pulled out her phone and searched for Officer Piper's number. Had she remembered to enter it? She remembered him giving her his card, telling her that there was an after-hours line that was manned twenty-four hours a day, even though there was no 9-1-1 service in Bald Eagle Falls. But she didn't know whether she had put the number into her contacts or not.

There was only one number listed for Officer Piper and she hadn't noted whether it was his office number or the 24-hour number. She pressed 'call' anyway and waited while the phone took its own sweet time connecting. She had two bars, so it should go through. Finally, she heard the ring tone and waited a bit more for the dispatcher to answer the call.

"Piper."

"Oh… is this your personal cell phone?" Erin was flummoxed and didn't know what to say.

"Yes. Who is this?"

"It's Erin Price. I meant to call the emergency number, but I must not have written it down. Can you tell me what it is?"

"They're just going to turn around and call me, I'm on call tonight. What's wrong?" His voice had taken on an edge.

"I'm at the bakery and I think… I think there's someone here. In the basement. The back door was open. Someone must have picked it or used an extra set of keys to get in."

"I told you to change the locks."

"I know, but the guy is on vacation…"

"Michael Fletcher is about as useful as a steering wheel on a mule. You should have called me, I would have lit a fire under him. I'll be at your store within five minutes. Don't go down to investigate. Go back outside to your car. Are you parked behind or in front?"

"Behind."

"Just wait for me. Don't try to do anything yourself. Even if the burglar comes back out, just stay in your car with the doors locked."

"Okay." Erin slipped back out the door. "I called out to them. That was probably a stupid thing to do. I was startled, it was just my first reaction."

"I'm hanging up so I can get over there. Just get in your car and wait."

"Okay."

Piper terminated the call and Erin slid the phone back into her purse. She got into the car and locked the doors, then sat looking at the back door, waiting for the intruder to come back out.

She didn't even see Piper at first. He had a dark car and crept down the back lane with no lights on. He pulled in behind her car. He and K9 got out and headed for the back door. Erin unlocked her door to get out and talk to him, but he motioned for her to stay put and entered the bakery, weapon drawn. It was like watching a TV drama with the sound off. Except that once he entered the building, there were no cameras following him, so she was left to imagine what was going on.

It had to be at least ten minutes before Piper returned to the car. He motioned for her to roll down her window. Erin did.

"Was there anyone there? Did you find anyone?"

"They were gone by the time I arrived. Out the front door. I'm sure it wasn't their preferred exit route, because they could have been seen out on the street, but knowing that you were at the back door, they didn't have much choice."

"Did you see them? Do you know who it was?"

"No." He frowned at her. "Why would someone be breaking into your store? We already searched it for evidence in Mrs. Plaint's murder. I can't think of a reason for anyone to be there, other than the thrill of visiting the site of a murder."

"Well..." Erin trailed off, trying to think of how to avoid telling him about her amateur investigation. "It could be that."

"Or...?"

"It could be the ghost. Seeing if they can catch a glimpse of my ghost."

"We both know that your ghost was Vic."

"But everybody in town doesn't know that. Just the three of us. We couldn't very well go around telling everyone that she'd been hiding out in my bakery."

"What else?" He was staring at her. As if he could see right into her brain and tell if she was lying.

"I might have said that there was a locked cabinet down there," Erin said slowly. "A mysterious locked cabinet that might hold the secret to a buried treasure. Or something."

"And why would you have said that?"

"I was trying to find out who might have keys from when Clementine was here. She apparently gave out a few of them and I wanted to track them all down. To help you out."

"So, you told people there was a locked cabinet."

"I thought if I said that I didn't have a key to it, but Clementine might have given a copy to someone with keys to the bakery... I might be able to find out who had keys to the bakery." It all sounded pretty lame to Erin when it came out of her mouth.

"And it didn't occur to you that people might want to investigate this mysterious cabinet with its clue to a buried treasure on their own? To beat you to the punch?"

"I didn't think it through. It was just spur of the moment."

"Why don't you leave the investigating to me?"

"Yeah. Sorry. It turns out there were a lot of keys floating around, though. If that helps you. Probably Mary Lou, and Melissa, and Gema. Angela herself. Maybe some of the other church ladies."

"We may never be able to trace them all. It seems like she gave out her keys pretty indiscriminately. The killer isn't going to tell us they have keys."

"No. I guess not. Did you find anything down there? Any clue as to who it was?"

"A crowbar. Like someone might use to pry open a locked cabinet."

"Oh." Erin remembered that Gema had suggested something like that. Which didn't mean it was Gema, of course. Melissa might have taken up her suggestion. Or someone else might have overheard, or had the same idea. It wasn't exactly proprietary technology.

"I'll need you to write up a statement. I'll get you the forms."

Erin nodded. Her evening wasn't over yet.

Piper went back to his car and returned with the statement forms for her to fill out.

"Are you actually after a buried treasure?" he inquired.

"Uh… no. Vic and I found a map at the house, to some caves and mines in the area, so that's why it was on my mind."

"Really." His lips pressed together grimly and Erin wondered what he was thinking.

"Yes… you sound like you don't believe me."

"You haven't exactly been forthcoming."

Erin thought she had been pretty up-front with him, so she wasn't sure what omission he was talking about. And she wasn't sure she wanted to know.

"We found an old map at Clementine's house. That's all."

"A geological map. What would she have a geological map for? She wasn't exactly in a business that required it. She didn't hike or climb. It's curious."

"Well, curious, yes. But not suspicious."

"I didn't say it was suspicious."

His expression and body language certainly had. But Erin couldn't argue with what he said. She turned on the car's dome light and bent over the witness statement to start filling it out.

"You're not planning on exploring any caves or mines?" Piper said, watching her.

"Uh… Vic wanted to go see a cave. She's picked one out on the map. We're not going to do anything adventurous. Just have a look around. Nothing that's too deep or requires special equipment."

He shook his head. "I wouldn't advise it. Some of those caves look perfectly safe, but have hidden hazards. If you want to see a cave, go see one of the touristy ones with guides and barriers. Not a random cave from the map."

"We'll be careful. I won't let Vic go into anything that I'm not sure of. And we'll be together, if something happens."

"You'll have to make sure it's on public land. You don't want to run afoul of some moonshiner with a shotgun because you've trespassed on his land."

Erin laughed, but then realized he was serious. "Are there really moonshiners around here still? I mean, prohibition ended long ago."

"Alcohol is regulated and there are unregulated stills operating in the mountains around here. You want to stay away from anything like that, because moonshiners can be very touchy about strangers."

"Okay. I'm not going to mess with anyone's still or trespass on private land. And we're not going to do anything dangerous."

Erin went back to writing her statement. But she gathered from the way Piper was hovering over her that he wasn't finished. She looked up at him.

"There are other things going on in the hills too. This may be the back country, but that doesn't mean there's no crime. The drug trade makes use of those large tracts of unmanaged land. There are growing fields, drug labs, stashes. It's not really safe to go poking around."

"You make it sound like the wild west. Or some ghetto. It's not really that bad, is it?"

"It's bad enough that I'm warning you."

"Okay… well… noted. I'll talk to Vic about it. Maybe I can convince her to go to a public admission cave instead."

He nodded. "Good."

Erin scratched out a few more words on the witness statement. "I was going to ask you about William Andrews."

"What about him?"

"Is he… okay? Is he a suspect?"

"Everyone is a suspect. Why William Andrews?"

"He was hanging around when I unloaded groceries before Angela died. He seems like sort of a shady character and I just wondered… it's possible he could have tampered with something. I can't imagine why or that Angela would have been his target, but it's a possibility."

"Hanging around how?"

"He was trying to help me carry things in. Grabbed one bag of flour when I asked him not to. He was still trying to help out after I told him not to. I eventually had to chase him off by threatening to call you."

"Did he have the opportunity to put something in the flour or any of the other ingredients?"

"I… don't think so. He'd have had to be quick and have planned ahead. But it was dark and my back was to him, and I was out of sight in the bakery for a few minutes. So, it is conceivable."

"But not likely."

"No… I don't see how he could have targeted Angela. But maybe it wasn't just targeted at her… do we know for sure now that it was an allergic reaction and not a poison?"

"That's what the coroner says," Piper said with a nod.

"So, it wasn't just a general toxin. Unless it's something that everyone is allergic to, like poison ivy."

"If it was poison ivy, everyone would have had a reaction. Not just Mrs. Plaint."

"Yeah… you're right. But even if he didn't contaminate something then, when he was trying to take my groceries in, that could have just been his first attempt. He could have tried and succeeded with something else later on."

"It's possible. Is there any indication that he might have had a key?"

"No. Just... I understand he does odd jobs around here. It's possible that he did some work for Clementine and had a key. Or was hired to maintain the place after she died."

"I'll have to make inquiries. I don't know if your aunt kept any financial records at home, but if she did, you could look through them and see if there were any check stubs to Mr. Andrews."

"Okay. I'll do that." Erin smothered a big yawn. "I'm beat. Can I finish this statement in the morning? I can barely put two thoughts together."

"Sure. Just drop it by the office." Piper gave a little frown, as if troubled.

"What is it? What are you thinking about?"

"Mm. Nothing. Just that Mr. Andrews is the courier we use to send evidence to the coroner."

"He has access to the evidence in this case?" Erin was horrified at the thought.

"No. Not access, exactly. Everything is sealed and the coroner would let me know if anything had been tampered with. But I might just ask them to do a full inventory, to make sure that all evidence was accounted for. It would be risky for Mr. Andrews to 'lose' anything along the way. Chances are the coroner would notice it was missing when comparing the log in sheet with the inventory sheet that was sent over. But sometimes, when there's a load of exhibits, it's easy to miss one and things do go missing."

"Why would you use someone like that as a courier?"

His brows drew down. "Someone like what?"

"Someone so..." Erin trailed off, realizing that she had adopted Angela's opinion of the man, as someone shiftless and lazy, a drifter. Someone to be suspicious of. But when she compared what she knew of the man firsthand, she realized there was nothing to back the opinion up. The man had volunteered to help her with her groceries, not asking for anything for doing it. She had seen him doing work for others. The police department used him as a courier. Every indication was that he was a busy, productive member of the community. "I don't know what I was thinking. I don't really know anything about him."

Piper nodded. "You can't judge people by their appearances," he reminded her.

And she was. "No. I'm sorry. I didn't even realize I was doing it."

He looked mollified by her apology.

"What exactly *does* he do?" Erin asked. "I mean other than acting as a courier and doing odd jobs? His skin... he looks like he does welding."

"He's a prospector of some sort. He keeps himself to himself, so I don't know the details. Some kind of mining out in the hills."

"Gold?"

"I said I don't know. He doesn't trade it in town. Whatever he digs out of the mountain he takes elsewhere for processing or sale."

Erin thought about his warnings about drug dealers working in the area. Could William Andrews be one of those drug dealers? If he were doing so many other odd jobs, it wasn't beyond the realm of possibility that he was involved in some stage of the drug trade.

Erin rubbed her forehead. "I'd better be going. Sorry to keep you. I feel sort of silly about calling you when I'd already scared the burglar off."

"Don't say that," Piper ordered. "You did the right thing. You never go into the building when you think there's been a break-in. These heroines on TV who just go waltzing in to investigate for themselves or confront a burglar, in real life they would be dead. You let me deal with it."

Erin gave him a little smile. "Okay, Officer Piper," she agreed. "I don't feel so bad, then."

"Bring that by the police department in the morning. Or when you take a break."

"I hear you had a burglar," Mary Lou said, startling Erin when she fell into step beside her on her way to the police department the next morning.

Erin put her hand over her heart to calm its rapid beating. "How did you hear that so soon?"

"Word spreads fast in a small town," Mary Lou said. "I think your young Vicky mentioned it to Mrs. Foster."

"Oh. Sure. Well, yes, somebody was in the basement when I went by to drop off some supplies."

Mary Lou shook her head, smiling. "That's what happens when you start spreading rumors of treasure maps and such. Best you keep your mouth shut about things you don't want anyone to know."

"Yes," Erin agreed. "You're right, of course. It was pretty stupid of me."

"Is that your report?" Mary Lou nodded to the pink form that Erin held clutched in her hand.

"Yes."

Mary Lou lifted her brows and made a small motion with her hand as if she expected Erin to hand it to her. Erin resisted her automatic impulse to hand it to her.

"Nothing too interesting, I'm afraid. I never saw who it was. They were out of there before I could see who it was."

Mary Lou's shoulders dipped a little. There was a slight relaxation of the muscles around her eyes. Erin tried not to react to these small indications. They didn't qualify as proof that Mary Lou had anything to do with the burglary and was relieved to find that she was not suspected. There might have been something else on her mind, or Erin might be completely misreading the signs, just seeing what she wanted to.

It was unnerving having the store broken into, even though nothing was damaged or stolen. Erin wanted to know who had done it. She felt vulnerable and angry at the same time.

"You don't have any idea who it could be?" she asked Mary Lou.

"Goodness, how would I? Everyone was talking about your treasure map and the missing key. It could have been anyone. Even someone from out of town."

"Not just anyone. Someone who had a key. The back door was unlocked."

Mary Lou's eyes flickered. "You might have left it unlocked by mistake."

"No, I didn't. Whoever broke in let themselves in with a key. Which means it was someone from town."

"I suppose it does. You didn't have any luck finding out who your aunt gave keys to…?"

"Some," Erin said. "But no one who has actually turned them in."

"I saw Fletcher on Main Street. I assume he's there to change out your locks?"

"Yes. I tried to get him to do it last week, but apparently he needs an order from the police to get into action."

Mary Lou gave a low chuckle. "He does sometimes need a little encouragement to get out to a job."

"We might have been able to avoid the burglary if he'd done it when I asked him to."

"Or if you hadn't spread the rumor that there was a mysterious locked cabinet in your basement."

Erin met Mary Lou's eyes. It was obvious Mary Lou knew that there was no locked cabinet. Was it because she had been there and seen for herself? Or had the burglar then spread the word that there was no such cabinet? Or maybe Mary Lou had been down in the basement before and knew it didn't exist? It was pretty obvious to anyone who had been downstairs that it held no secrets. There was no cabinet, no safe, no mysterious locked door. Just a small bathroom and storeroom.

"If you want to keep a secret in Bald Eagle Falls, you have to be pretty savvy," Mary Lou offered. "There aren't a lot of secrets here."

Erin chewed on the inside of her lip. It seemed to her that there *were* a lot of secrets in Bald Eagle Falls. A lot of things that were kept secret from Erin, at any rate. Maybe to a long-time resident like Mary Lou, it was different. She would know who to talk to and would have the trust of the gossip-mongers. But they were more likely to talk *about* Erin than *to* her.

"Secrets like what happened to Angela's husband and son?" she suggested.

Mary Lou's eyes widened. She put her hand on Erin's arm, stopping her. They were only a few steps from the civic center. Mary Lou obviously wanted to continue the conversation beyond what they could discuss before reaching Officer Piper's door.

"How did you hear about that?" she demanded in a hushed tone.

"Someone was telling me how Angela's husband disappeared without a trace. And then later, in his graduating year, her son. Same thing. Just disappeared into thin air."

"Nobody disappears into thin air."

"Does that mean someone knows something about it?"

Mary Lou considered this for some time. "Somebody always knows something. And in a little town like this, probably more people than you would expect know something."

"Does that mean *you* know what happened to them?"

Mary Lou's hand dropped away from Erin's arm.

"I do not." Her voice was crisp and firm, devoid of emotion. "I know nothing about what happened to them and I don't want to know. The family was apparently much more dysfunctional than it appeared to be in public. Angela always appeared to have things in control. But there are some things you just can't hold on to. The harder you try, the more they squirm away."

"Like secrets?"

"Like I said, secrets are hard to keep in a small town like this. Even if you lie to cover them up, people still figure it out. You try to cover it up, but someone sees. Someone hears. Someone knows."

Erin gave a little shiver in spite of the heat of the day.

"*Who* knows?" she asked. Was Mary Lou trying to give her a warning? Or a clue?

There was a period of silence from Mary Lou while she considered her answer. Erin had decided that she wasn't going to answer, and then Mary Lou spoke. Her voice was low.

"Angela was the type of person who always knew. Always figured things out. Trying to keep a secret around her was like… trying to hold on to the wind. Somehow, she always knew things that were best left alone."

"Did she know things about you?"

"Honey, I don't have any secrets. It's all out there. Everybody knows my business. I don't try to cover it up. But other people. Most people have something they would rather keep private. An indiscretion. A secret addiction. A mask that they wear…"

Erin thought of the people around her and, in particular, the suspects in Angela's murder. If Angela was someone who collected other people's secrets, that made her a target to a lot more people than just Erin or Vic. Erin's and Vic's motives were tiny in comparison to secrets that other people might be desperate to keep from public view.

"Was Angela a blackmailer? Is that what you mean? Did she make people pay her to keep quiet?"

"Of course not. Nothing so crass. But she had other ways of manipulating people. Getting what she wanted from them. A little twist here, a nudge there. A word or two dropped at a time when only her target would understand. You can understand how someone who wanted to protect their reputation could become… hostile."

"Do you know who wanted to hurt her?"

Mary Lou looked back the direction they had come. "I shouldn't have said anything."

"Do you? Do you know who wanted to hurt her? Who would want to kill her?"

There was only silence for a reply.

"Mary Lou!"

"A lot of people wanted to put a stop to what Angela was doing."

"You?" Erin could hear the malice in Mary Lou's normally calm, cultured voice. "What did she do to you?"

Mary Lou looked down at her watch, then ran her hand over her hair, smoothing it. "I'm afraid I can't chat any longer. You can get my story from anyone in town. Like I said, it's all out there. I don't have any secrets."

Erin reached out to delay Mary Lou, but the gesture was pointless; Mary Lou had already turned away from her and was walking away at a quick pace, her heels clicking down the sidewalk. Erin watched her go. There was so much hate and anger toward Angela; it seemed that the surprise wasn't that she had died, but that she had survived for so long in the first place.

She went on to the police department and looked in on the offices where she had previously met Terry Piper. He was not there, but there was an unfamiliar woman typing at one of the computers. She looked up and nodded at the form clutched in Erin's hand.

"Witness statement?" she asked briskly. "In the bin over there." She nodded to a tray on the corner of the desk that was neatly labeled 'forms to be processed' and contained a few other varicolored papers waiting to be dealt with.

"Thank you." Erin put it down and looked at the woman, awkward and unsure what else to say.

"You must be Erin Price."

"Yes. I don't think we've met?"

"Nope. Clara Jones."

"Uh… nice to meet you."

"So, you run the new bakery." Clara was a middle-aged woman with brassy red hair and large earrings. She seemed out of place in a police department, but seemed to be comfortable there and acted as if she knew what she was doing. Erin remembered that Melissa had said she worked there as well, transcribing reports for Officer Piper.

"Yes. I hope you'll stop by. You missed opening day, but I'll give you a free muffin."

"I'm sure they're good for gluten-free. But I don't eat that kind of crap."

"Uh…" Erin wasn't sure whether it was 'crap' because it was gluten-free or because it was full of processed flour and sugar, and decided that either way, she didn't want to take it up with Clara. "Sure. Well, any time."

"I don't know what you're still doing in town," Clara said, pausing in her typing to pick up her mug and take a sip of coffee. "If it was me, and I was accused of murder, I wouldn't be sticking around for them to pin it on me. Nobody wanted another bakery in town, and with Angela Plaint's murder… if it was me, I'd sell the business and pack up."

"I can't really leave," Erin protested. "Not while it's still being investigated."

"You stay around here stirring up trouble like you have been and you'll be the next one on a slab in the city. Don't you know how you're upsetting people?"

"Stirring up trouble? What did I do?"

"Asking questions. Stirring up the past that is best left undisturbed. What business is it of yours?"

"It's my business because I'm the one who's been accused of murder! You expect me to just tuck my tail between my legs and run away? Maybe that's how people handle things here in Bald Eagle Falls, but like you say, I'm not from around here. And that's not how I'm going to act. I'm not going to pull a disappearing act. I have just as much of a right to live here and to run my business as anyone else."

"Sometimes people don't leave of their own free choice," Clara said cryptically.

"Clara." Terry Piper's voice came from behind Erin, making her jump.

Clara had been looking at her computer screen and obviously hadn't seen Piper approaching. She took another sip of her coffee, hiding her face behind the big mug. "Miss Price brought in her witness statement," she said, indicating the pink page at the top of the basket to be processed. "About the *alleged* burglary of her shop by someone looking for an *alleged* buried treasure."

Erin opened her mouth to retort, but Piper spoke over her.

"Good. We need to get that into the computer as soon as possible. It's important to stay on top of these reports."

"Yes, sir," Clara agreed, her voice light and unconcerned. "Anything else?"

"No, it's been pretty quiet. Barking dog complaint from Mrs. Snell. Mr. Timon asking for the latest on the Plaint murder for an update in the paper."

"I'll deal with those later." Piper motioned to Erin. "I'll walk you back to the bakery."

"I think I'm pretty safe," Erin retorted. She looked at Clara. "It isn't like anyone is trying to kill me."

"Come." He grasped her upper arm lightly and steered her back out of the office. He didn't speak until they got out to the sidewalk and started heading back to the bakery. K9 kept pace at Piper's side. "Too many loose lips in Bald Eagle Falls," he said. "I wish we had a bigger pool to draw on for administrative help at the office. But there really aren't that many people who are interested. The help that we do get is too... undisciplined."

"It's a bit of a shock living in such a small town. I thought I had lived in some little places before, but by Bald Eagle Falls standards, they were huge. Here… everybody really does know everybody else's business, don't they?"

"There are plenty of people who are happy to spread it."

They walked for a couple of minutes in silence. "I hear that Angela was someone who knew everyone's business," Erin ventured.

"I don't know that she was any worse than anyone else."

"From what I've heard… it sounds like she was blackmailing half the town."

Piper chuckled. "Now that she's not around to defend herself. That's pretty blatant gossip. I don't have any evidence she was blackmailing anyone."

"Maybe not blackmailing," Erin said, "I don't mean she was demanding to be paid. But… manipulating people, threatening to expose them."

Piper frowned, shaking his head. "I haven't heard anything like that. I'm not sure how to prove something like that."

"Maybe she had pictures of people, or recordings or letters…"

"Nothing in her possessions. We've already searched through them." He caught her glance at him. "What?"

"Who is *we*? You and K9?"

K9 looked up when he heard his name. He let out a whine.

"I'm not the only person in the police department. We have the Sheriff. And Tom Banks is the other officer, but he is only part time, called in as we need him. All three of us searched Mrs. Plaint's house. I can assure you, there was no evidence she was keeping dirt on anyone."

Erin sighed and nodded.

"I am investigating Mrs. Plaint's death, Miss Price. You seem to think that I'm just a country bumpkin and don't have any idea what to do with a murder investigation, but I can assure you I'm fully qualified and I have federal resources to draw upon."

"You could call me Erin."

He gazed at her for a moment, his eyes deep, dark pools. "No. I don't think I can. I need to maintain a certain level of professionalism."

Erin thought about what he had said. "I believe that you're investigating," she said. "It just seems backward that you're focusing on the two people who are from out of town, when it seems more likely someone who knew her well would have a motive to harm her. What motive would I have? You really think I would kill someone because they were a competitor?"

"People have killed for less."

"I didn't kill Angela Plaint because I want a monopoly on Bald Eagle Falls's bakery business."

He shrugged. "Okay."

"Okay?"

"You had the best means and opportunity. But I admit that your motive is not as strong as others'. Vic's, for instance."

"Vic didn't kill Angela."

"How much do you really know about Vic?"

He turned his gaze on her. Erin looked away uncomfortably, not wanting to give anything away.

"I know she didn't kill Angela."

"You hope she didn't. You don't *know* anything about her."

"I know what kind of person she is. She's been living and working with me. I know she's not a killer." She turned back toward Piper and stared at his nose. She couldn't meet his eyes, but she knew he wouldn't be able to tell the difference as long as she was close. She had promised Vic she wouldn't tell him about her past unless asked directly and she intended to keep that promise. She needed to give him the impression that she had told him everything she knew. That she was trustworthy. "I'm a good judge of character."

Piper continued to look at her. "Do you know that's not her real name?"

Erin swallowed. "Yes."

"Really. What is her real name?"

"You'd have to ask her."

"Did you know she's not Angela Plaint's niece?"

"Angela was her aunt," Erin said firmly.

He considered this, then shrugged. Aunt could mean different things to different people. It didn't always mean there was a blood or legal connection. Sometimes an aunt was your mother's best friend, or a godmother or cherished babysitter. Or a cousin who happened to be a generation older.

"You can let her know that I need to talk to her again. Go over a few things in her statement." He looked at his watch. "I know you're getting ready for the lunch rush, so I won't expect to see her right now. But I'd like to talk to her again soon."

Chapter Thirteen

KNOWING THAT THEY WERE going to be working Sunday morning and that they were going to need a little bit of equipment for their trip to the cave after the women's tea, Vic and Erin closed up shop early Saturday afternoon and took Erin's car to the city.

Vic seemed much more anxious in the city than in Bald Eagle Falls. Erin caught her looking around the camping gear store nervously, as if she were expecting to be attacked or accused of something.

"What's wrong?" Erin asked. "Did Officer Piper tell you not to leave town?" she teased.

"Well, he did, but I told him we'd be coming here. He said that was okay, as long as I was going to be around and would make myself available for questioning."

"It was a joke. I didn't know he had really told you that."

"I know." Vic turned all the way around, like a searchlight sweeping the darkness for some hidden danger. "I know you like him, but I don't like having to answer all his questions. He's nice enough about it, but I know he suspects me. He thinks I killed Aunt Angela."

"We'll have to just keep asking questions and pushing him to look in other directions. As long as he keeps looking, he'll find out who it was sooner or later."

But she knew that the disappearances of Angela's husband and son had never been solved. Who had the police been at that point? It would have been too long ago for it to have been Officer Piper. Then again, Melissa wouldn't necessarily have had all the details. She hadn't been transcribing police reports back then. She had only been seventeen when Angela's son disappeared. And younger when Angela's husband left. The police might have tracked both of them down. Might have satisfied themselves that there was nothing to be concerned about, that they simply hadn't wanted to be with Angela anymore. A man was entitled to leave if he wanted to. Plenty of men did, and never contacted their families again.

Still, it worried her. Maybe crimes weren't so easily solved in Bald Eagle Falls.

"What are you so nervous about?" she asked Vic, getting back around to the original question.

"I don't want anyone to see me who might know me. From before. I don't want to run into any old friends or neighbors. Or worse, family. Or somebody who knows my mom and is going to run back and tell her all about seeing me here. Like this." Vic slid her fingers through her smooth blond ponytail, frowning.

"You look lovely," Erin assured her. "If anyone recognizes you... well, we'll just deal with that. What's your mom going to do? She already kicked you out. You're not in contact with her. What does it matter what she hears or thinks?"

"Yeah." Vic bit her lip. "You're right. I just can't help feeling..."

"It will be okay. We'll handle it. Nothing bad is going to happen."

"Okay."

They went on with their shopping, referring to the equipment list that Vic had compiled. Erin couldn't believe how eager the girl was to explore some caves. Erin felt anxious just thinking about it, but Vic was all-in. She wanted to be crawling through dark tunnels, miles underground, where there was no telling when you might fall off of a cliff, into an underground lake, or just asphyxiate from lack of oxygen.

"We're not going anywhere dangerous," Erin. "Nothing that's really far underground. We're both just beginners."

"I know." Vic gave her a grin, laughing at Erin's anxiety now. "But even beginners need flashlights and safety equipment. Just the basics."

"It seems like an awfully long list for just the basics."

"That's all it is. I just went by beginner lists."

"What else?"

"Uh..." Vic looked down at her neat, concise printing. "Rope."

"Rope? Why do we need rope? We're not going to fall down anywhere."

"Just to be safe. Just for emergencies."

"No emergencies. I'm not going to any caves if we're going to have emergencies."

"We won't. It's just on the list. So, we get it."

Erin grumbled while Vic searched through the spools of rope to find the kind that she wanted. An employee cut it to the specified length and finished the ends. Vic added it to the shopping cart.

"Oh, look who it is!"

Vic's head whipped around and she followed Erin's pointing finger to see Gema. She breathed a sigh of relief. "Don't scare me like that!"

"I'm sorry. I wouldn't know any of your family or friends anyway. The only people I know around here are from Bald Eagle Falls."

"Oh. Right."

They were both watching as Gema spoke to another woman, a little younger than she was. She was closer to Erin in size and body shape and, unlike Gema's iron-gray waves, she had close-cropped, spiky red hair. The two women were too far away for Erin and Vic to hear what they were saying.

The other woman had on the green vest of a store employee, but Gema didn't seem to be looking for anything. They were just having a friendly conversation. Gema's fingertips rested on the clerk's arm, as if stopping her from leaving.

"These little towns," Vic said. "You can never go anywhere without running into someone you know. Even when you go into the city."

"I suppose. I haven't lived anywhere as small as Bald Eagle Falls before."

"Compasses."

"What?" Erin looked down at the shelf display of compasses. "Do we need anything special? Maybe we should get a GPS. Do they make GPSs for caving? They make those little fish radar things for fishing, is there anything like that for mapping out the tunnels in case you get lost?"

Vic rolled her eyes. "There is no GPS or radar for caving. You need a compass."

"You're the one who has been doing the research. You pick one out."

As Vic looked through the compasses and compared features and prices and how they felt in her hand, Erin watched Gema and the store clerk. Eventually, they said their goodbyes and gave each other a hug. They separated to go their different directions. Erin waved to catch Gema's attention.

"Gema! Over here!"

Gema turned her head, obviously catching Erin's voice. Then Gema spotted her. She looked hesitant at first, looking toward the exit doors of the camping store as if she had to leave. Then she turned back toward Erin and moved toward them, smiling.

"What are you guys doing here?" she asked. "Doing some camping?"

"Spelunking," Vic declared, at the same time as Erin said, "Caving."

Erin shook her head. "Fine. Spelunking," she agreed. "But no underground lakes."

"That sounds like fun," Gema said. "Where are you going? There are some nice ones around here."

"Erin found a map—"

"Oh, yes. Your map." Gema laughed. "Treasure hunting, then?"

"I wouldn't mind if we found some treasure," Vic said.

"We're not looking for treasure," Erin disagreed. "We're just going to look at a couple of caves. Nothing too remote or scary. Just some well-traveled, safe caves."

"I looked at the map and picked a couple out," Vic contributed, ignoring Erin. "And I looked them up on Google Maps and made sure that none of them are big commercial places. There are a couple of small ones that I couldn't even find on Google Maps, so I don't know if they've had a cave-in, or what—"

"Cave-in?" Erin echoed weakly. It was sounding like a worse and worse idea. What were they thinking, going to explore caves where there was no one else to help them? Two inexperienced women, alone. Probably GPS and cell phones wouldn't even work out there in the sticks. They could be lost for days.

"We won't go into one that has had a cave-in," Vic assured her. But that wasn't what Erin wanted to hear. She wanted to hear that they wouldn't go anywhere near any of the remote, non-tourist caves.

Erin looked at Gema for help. "Have you ever done this? Explored a cave?"

"Sure. I grew up in the area. I've been in a lot of caves around here. Even used to take my boys to some of them. Boys love exploring caves."

"Maybe we should get Gema to go with us," Erin suggested to Vic. "That would be okay, wouldn't it?"

Vic's face fell. "I wanted it to be just the two of us." She looked at Gema. "I don't mean anything by it, I just wanted to do something ourselves."

"Of course I'm not offended. If you want to explore caves together, that's what you should do. People should do what makes them happy." She looked wistful. Erin wondered if she was thinking about her family and how they used to explore together. Now it was just Gema and her husband. Erin had seen the two of them together, but Gema's husband didn't match her for vibrancy. He looked more like the type of husband to fall asleep with a beer in front of the TV than someone who would go on adventures with her. And maybe that was fine with Gema. But she did look like she was missing the fun they had had when they were raising their boys together.

"So, what brings you here?" Erin asked. She made a motion to where Gema had been talking with her friend. "Was that—"

"A young cousin of mine. I always see how she's doing when I'm in the area."

On considering, Erin thought there had been similarities in their features.

Gema looked at the compasses on the shelf. "Do these ever bring back memories." She tapped one. "Did you know that Mary Lou and I were in Girl Guides together? A coon's age ago, to be sure. Can you believe we've known each other for that long?"

"Wow," Vic said. "I haven't known anyone that long."

"You haven't been alive that long!" Erin laughed. "I haven't either, though. I moved around so much... I haven't known anyone more than a couple of years."

"Really?" Gema shook her head. "That would be very strange to me. I've lived in Bald Eagle Falls all my life. I'm practically a fixture."

Vic finally picked out a couple of compasses and showed them to Gema, the experienced one. "These ones? Do you think they're good?"

"Those ones will be just fine."

"Mary Lou said something funny the other day," Erin said, thinking back.

"What was she talking about?"

"She was talking about Angela." Erin glanced at Vic to make sure she didn't mind Erin talking about her aunt in front of her. Vic gave a little nod. "She was saying that Angela was the type of person who knew everything about everyone. Even the things they wanted to keep secret."

Gema raised her brows.

"And she would hold what she knew over people to make them do what she wanted them to. Like... emotional blackmail."

"I wouldn't know anything about that," Gema said. She gave a little laugh and swept her hair back behind her head with both hands, looking like she was going to scrunch it all together into a ponytail. Then she released it. "What *exactly* was Mary Lou talking about?"

"I don't know. She didn't give any specific examples. She just said that everyone had secrets... and Angela knew them all."

"I see."

"But she said she didn't have any," Erin continued. "She said her life is an open book; she doesn't hide anything. When I asked her about what happened between her and Angela, she said I should ask someone else about it. Why it was Mary Lou didn't like her."

Gema shook her head. "That's a long story. Well, not so much a long story as a sad one. A tragedy."

"Really?" Erin added the compasses to the shopping cart. She was hoping they were at the end of Vic's list and could start to head for the check-out. Vic folded the list up, which Erin took as a signal they were done. She turned the cart around and pointed it toward the check out lines. "So, what happened?"

"Angela was always involved in these new businesses and ideas. She was a good businessperson, she always made back her investment. She was very sharp."

"I heard that."

"That is, she always made her investment back... until she didn't."

"What does that mean?"

"She got Mary Lou and half the town involved in some scheme. One of these things where everyone is supposed to get back ten times what they put into it. If it sounds too good to be true, it probably is. That's what I always said."

"How did Angela get Mary Lou into something so risky? She seems so level-headed."

"I don't know. Just because Angela was Angela. It always worked out. So, why wouldn't it work out again? It was more risky, but that just meant that it was going to bring in a better return."

They waited in line for a cashier. Erin could already see how the story was going to end.

"She always made her investment back. Until she didn't."

Gema nodded. "Mary Lou went all-in. She put everything she had into the scheme. And more. She borrowed."

"Oh, no..."

"Yes. When everything came crashing down... Angela had only invested modestly. Some people had been careful and some had risked more. But Mary Lou... she had been sure it was her chance to put away enough for retirement. Maybe even an early retirement. They had never been wealthy. Her husband, Roger, he was a plodder."

"She must have been crushed."

"Mary Lou is made of pretty stern stuff. She declared bankruptcy. Promised all her creditors that she was still going to pay them back, no matter how long it took. Started working, which she hadn't done since before the boys were born. But Roger couldn't handle it. The way that he'd been embarrassed in front of everyone he knew. Losing the house and his car. The way that people talked about them."

"What did he do?"

"He tried to take his own life, of course. And failed at that too."

Erin swallowed and nodded. She didn't know what else to say, or if it were acceptable to ask for more information.

"He has a brain injury from going without oxygen," Gema said matter-of-factly. "And, of course, he still suffers from depression. Not just over the money, but now about what he's done to himself and his family, too. He completely failed them. And he put all of that burden on his wife and sons."

Her words made Erin feel the horrible bleakness herself. They had lost everything. And his attempt to escape it all had just made it that much worse.

"Mary Lou is always so cheerful," she said in amazement. "You'd never guess by looking at her that any of this had happened! And she doesn't look…" Erin struggled for a tactful way to say it and failed, "…poor. She always looks so perfectly turned-out."

"And those boys are the same way. You'd never guess there was anything wrong at home. They're all-stars at school. They work part time to help support the family. And they're like her, always cheerful and not letting anyone feel sorry for them."

"That's amazing. It really is."

Vic had been silent throughout the story. After the cashier finished ringing everything through, Erin paid with her credit card. She'd always done her best to master the situation and pull herself out of the holes she ended up in. But Mary Lou reached a whole new level with the way she dealt with her troubles.

Gema smiled a polite goodbye. "I still have some errands to run before going back to Bald Eagle Falls. I'm sure I'll see you girls there."

"You're coming by for tea after church tomorrow, right?" Erin verified.

"Yes. I'll be there. We'll all be there."

Vic helped Erin to load their gear into the car, quiet and contemplative. Erin looked at her as they sat down in front and put their seat-belts on.

"Are you okay?"

"Just thinking."

"About Mary Lou?"

"I thought I had things tough. You know, I get myself down and sit around feeling sorry for what I've been through. And then I hear something like this… and I realize, I'm still such a baby. Not because I'm young, but because… what I've gone through is nothing compared to what someone like Mary Lou had been through. Losing everything, including her house. Her husband. His wage-earning ability. It's just… it's so sad. What happened to me? I got called names. I got kicked out. So, what? I still have the ability to make money and learn to support myself. I have a friend who gave me work and a place to live until I get on my feet. I really have everything I could want."

Erin nodded her agreement. "Same for me. I mope around about how I didn't have any parents. Had to grow up in foster homes. Had to fend for myself when I was eighteen, and pretty much for a couple of years before that. I was working as soon as I was old enough to get a job, because I knew I was going to have to look after myself. And… so what? Now I'm independent. I'm strong. I have my own business and an employee. And a cat. I'm not tied down to a disabled husband and two children. I don't have thousands of dollars in debt to pay back. Mary Lou would probably love to have all the advantages that I do."

"Yeah."

Erin blew out her breath in a sigh. "It just puts everything in perspective."

"Even being a murder suspect. It isn't like they've arrested me and put me behind bars. Things could be a lot worse."

"Just be glad we didn't live back in the days when they would just string you up. No judge or jury, no investigation or human rights. Someone thinks you did it, and they hang you."

They drove in silence for a while.

"We're still going to the caves, right?"

Erin laughed. "We're still going to the caves. But you better make sure I don't die there."

Sunday morning they slept in, and it was heavenly. God or no god, Erin awoke with a prayer of thanks in her heart for the extra hours of sleep. And that Orange Blossom had let them sleep in and not started howling for his breakfast.

Since all they were doing was tea and not opening up the bakery for a full shopping day, they just had a few items to put in the oven and had prepared it all ahead of time so that all they needed was a couple of hours before church let out. Then the church ladies made their way down Main Street and set the front door bell ringing as they gathered in the chairs to gossip and relax. Erin had tea steeping—several varieties, in fact. The smells threw her back into the past, to Clementine's Tea Room. The smells and flavors of the teas that Clementine had carried were so familiar. Erin remembered all the old boxes and wrappers. And the women chattering away happily while little Erin carefully carried cookies and other treats to the tables.

"Erin, this is lovely," Mary Lou said, taking one slim biscotti biscuit from her tray. "Just like when Clementine was around. I hadn't even realized how much I have missed it. She was forced to retire because of her health. Certainly none of us ever held that against her. She just did what she had to do. But I have *missed* this."

There were nods from the other women and choruses of agreement from the sipping and munching clientele.

"There's nothing like sisterhood," Gema declared. She had a blueberry muffin with her tea, light-colored with the addition of plenty of cream. Erin didn't know all of the women well, but the faces were familiar and Erin had to agree with what Gema said about sisterhood. She felt warm and comfortable and secure. All her anxiety evaporated with the steam from the tea.

"You really should join us at church too," Melissa said. "We had a really nice service today."

The other ladies quieted, looking at each other and looking at Erin out the corners of their eyes, not daring to meet her gaze.

"Thank you," Erin said. "But I don't have any plans to go to church in the near future."

"And... what about you, Vic?" Melissa asked. "You're not an atheist too, are you? Did the two of you *not go* to the same church back in Maine?" She laughed at her own joke.

"No, I'm Christian... but God and I aren't exactly on good terms these days," Vic said haltingly.

There were a few minutes of awkward silence. Vic hovered, offering treats and coffee refills to anyone who appeared to be getting low. Erin didn't know what to do with her hands or how to get the conversation flowing smoothly again. If she bombed the first ladies' tea, there wouldn't be any point in trying it again. She could forget about bringing in any business on a Sunday.

"We're going exploring this afternoon," Vic offered brightly.

"Exploring? Exploring what?" One of the ladies immediately took up the thread.

"Caves. I have a map and I picked out a couple near here that look like they could be interesting. We picked up some gear yesterday and we're going to explore this afternoon!"

"How adventurous," Mary Lou said. She looked off into the distance. "We had some wonderful adventures when the boys were young. There was always somewhere new to explore. Now with the new geocaching, it seems like the young people are staying closer to home, picking out the easy walks instead of delving into the unexplored."

"Geocaching? They even do that in the city," Erin said. "There are a lot of urban caches; I had friends who did that."

"It's a great way to get out and be active," Melissa declared.

"But at the expense of *real* treasure hunting and exercise," Mary Lou pointed out.

"Maybe it's just one step along the way. Maybe if they start with geocaching, they'll get into more challenging stuff later."

Mary Lou sniffed. "I doubt it. People are happier to play games in front of the computer these days."

"What cave you going to?" Gema asked.

Erin looked at Vic, who was the one in charge of their adventure. She didn't know where the caves were that Vic had picked out. But Vic didn't answer.

"It's kind of... a secret," she said.

There were some giggles from the ladies, but they looked at Vic indulgently.

"Well... let me give you some advice." Gema said. "There are a couple of caves about ten miles north of town, near Beaver Creek."

Vic nodded, blinking. "Yeah, I saw those."

"Stay away from them."

Vic looked at Erin, then back at Gema. "They looked like they would be good."

"I've seen that shiftless William Andrews out there, messing around."

"He's just prospecting, isn't he?" Erin asked. "That's what Officer Piper said."

"Terry Piper doesn't know what's going on under his own nose."

"I hear he's a treasure hunter," Melissa said.

"Officer Piper?"

"No, William Andrews. He's searching those caves for Confederate gold."

"He's not looking for ore or for treasure," Gema disagreed, shaking her head at both of them. "He's a drug runner. He's got a stash out there."

Just like Officer Piper had warned Erin about. Despite what Gema thought, Piper did know there were drug runners using the caves. Not the specifics, maybe, but generally speaking.

"How do you know William Andrews is using the caves by Beaver Creek?" Erin asked Gema.

"I told you, I've seen him."

"Did you report it to the police department? I would think that if they knew something that specific, they would arrest him."

Gema laughed. "They have to catch him in the act and he's too canny for that. And those caves are like a labyrinth, you could wander down there for days and not find where he had hidden the drugs. And that's if you knew they were down there. A police investigation won't do much more than look in the mouth of the cave, or maybe a couple of the nearby passages if he's feeling adventurous. Searching every little crack and crevice? Not likely."

Erin didn't like the sound of labyrinthine caves, even if William Andrews wasn't using those caves for his nefarious business. "We'll find another cave to explore," she said to Vic. "Okay?"

Vic didn't look happy about it, but she nodded. "I have another one in mind."

Chapter Fourteen

RIN WOKE UP IN blackness. Her head was pounding and when she shifted her position, a wave of nausea washed over her. She tried to force her way through the fog in her brain to remember where she was or how she had gotten there. She was lying on her back.

Was it time to get up and start her baking?

She couldn't hear her alarm or see her clock, so she decided it was not.

She wanted to put her hand up to rub her head, but she couldn't seem to control her hand properly so she gave up

She wasn't sure if her eyes were open or closed. Everything hurt. It was quiet and dark, so she went to sleep.

The next time she awoke, she knew she had been lying there for a long time. It had to be time to get up. She tried to turn her head to look at the clock. The pain that ripped through her head like a knife left her gasping with shock and pain.

What had happened?

She was cold down to her bones.

The darkness hadn't lifted at all.

Without moving again, she evaluated her position. She wasn't lying in bed, like she had initially assumed. She was lying on something hard and gravelly. Had she slipped and fallen in the back alley?

Without turning her head, she tried to open her eyes and look around her. But her eyes were already open and she couldn't see a spark of light. No streetlights, no stars, nothing.

She was blind, then.

The pain in her head and the blindness meant that she had fallen and hit her head. She'd hurt herself badly.

Had she left the shop to put out the garbage, and had slipped and fallen?

Erin floated in and out of consciousness, unable to focus on a single thought.

She couldn't have slipped and fallen at the store. If she had, then Vic would have come looking for her.

She could kill you in your sleep.

Piper had warned her more than once.

You don't know anything about her.

Vic was the prime suspect in a murder investigation. There was a reason for that. Rejected by her favorite aunt because of her gender identity, Vic had retaliated. She had plotted to kill her aunt or had been surprised by her while hiding in the basement and somehow been able to trigger an allergic reaction. She had taken away Angela's autoinjector. The tall, strong girl would have easily overpowered her older, unwell aunt, either before or after an allergic reaction.

Erin could hear Vic's words in her head. *It was easy.*

It wasn't Vic. Erin's brain rebelled against the idea. Vic was a gentle, nonviolent person. Whenever she had spoken about Angela, it had been with sadness, not anger. The voice in her head could not be Vic's. It was someone else.

Because she *had* heard those words.

It was easy.

She was becoming more convinced that she had not fallen down outside of the shop. She had been hit. But it didn't feel like she was lying in the parking lot. She lay on a surface that was as hard as rock, but not as flat as the parking lot behind her building. There were loose bits of rock on top of the surface.

But the air was too still. And it was too dark. She had to be inside.

Why would there be rocks inside?

Erin tried to wet her lips, but her mouth was as dry as cotton and she couldn't work up any spit. Her lips were sore and cracked. She tried calling out anyway.

"Hello? Is there anybody there?"

Her voice was weak and odd in her own ears. Why did she sound like that?

The room was large, like a cathedral. Her voice, as quiet as it was, echoed off of the hard walls. Was it possible she was in a church? Paved inside with large flagstones, built out of rock? Why would she be in such a place?

Her face felt like a mask. Like it was made of thin plastic pulled taut. She could feel a pull on her skin whenever she moved her mouth.

There was a warm, foul smell in the still air.

"Hello?" she tried again.

There was no answering voice. All she could hear was her own trembling words and the voice in her head. The one who said it had been easy. Killing Angela had been easy, like squashing a particularly disgusting bug.

Erin tried again to move. Not her head, because that was too painful. Not her hands, since they didn't seem to follow her instructions properly. She stretched out one booted toe to prod first at the air and then at the wall beside her, trying to sense what she could about its shape.

It was rough and irregular. But she could tell little more through her boot.

Why was she wearing boots?

The darkness again became overwhelming. She had to fight back the urge to throw up. There was a dizzying swirl of vertigo and she passed out again.

She was in a cave.

That was what came to her the next time she surfaced. It was cold and dark and hard with vaulted ceilings. A cave. Buried somewhere underground.

She couldn't remember how she had gotten there.

Where was Vic? If Erin was there, Vic must also be there, somewhere beside her in the darkness.

"Vic? Vic, are you there?"

Her voice echoed again. But there was no answer. Erin squirmed around, looking for some sign of light. Listening for Vic's breath in the darkness.

Nothing.

How could she be there without Vic?

They had become separated. Had they made different turns down a labyrinthine tunnel? Had Erin fallen over a cliff and Vic had gone back for help?

Vic couldn't have hurt Erin. She was sure of that. The voice still buzzed in her head. *It was easy*. But it wasn't Vic's voice. Erin couldn't be sure whose it was. She had met so many new people since arriving at Bald Eagle Falls. She couldn't recognize all their voices.

"Vic? Victoria? Are you there? Can you hear me?"

Shouting took a lot of effort and Erin was left panting afterward. Was she low on oxygen? Were there heavy gases in the chamber, replacing the oxygen in her lungs with something her body couldn't use? Erin moved her shoulders, feeling for a backpack of equipment. She couldn't remember whether they had agreed to get small oxygen canisters or not. Vic had wanted to be prepared, but Erin had insisted that they'd better not be going anywhere dangerous. They didn't need oxygen if they were sticking close to the surface in well-ventilated caves. Who had won? Had Erin given in and paid for oxygen, just in case?

It didn't matter, because she didn't seem to have any gear. If she'd had a backpack when she entered the cave, she had somehow become separated from it. Lost it going over that cliff, maybe. Or maybe she had put it down while they had a snack and something had happened to distract her from putting it back on again.

Erin blinked her eyes, trying to keep herself awake. But it was impossible. The periods of sleep or unconsciousness were frequent, her periods of consciousness brief. She bit the inside of her cheek. She could barely feel it. She tried to pinch herself, but her hands were not working.

When she awoke again, Erin concentrated on her hands. Why were they not working? Had she put them out to catch herself when she fell, breaking her arms? It didn't seem likely. The worst pain in her head was in the back, not the top or the front. Surely if she landed on her hands, she would have broken her nose. But the goose-egg was on the back.

She had movement. Left, right, up, down, in, out. Her fingers seemed to be opening and shutting, though they were numb with cold, so she couldn't be one hundred percent sure.

"Then what's wrong?" Erin demanded out loud, trying to force her brain to process the problem and come up with a solution.

She moved them again. Left, right, up, down, in, out, wiggle.

She tried moving just her right hand, but her left stayed with it. She tried moving just her left, but her right moved in parallel. When she tried to pull them apart, she only got resistance and she couldn't separate them.

Erin closed her eyes. What did that mean? What did it mean if her hands would only move together, never apart?

It took a long time for the answer to make its way to the surface.

Her hands were tied together.

And that couldn't be an accident. She hadn't fallen over a cliff and tied her hands together. Somebody else had tied her hands together. They weren't splinted. It wasn't because she was injured. Someone had tied her up.

Erin tried moving her feet. Similar to her arms, she had a range of motion, but they stuck stubbornly together. Her ankles were also tied together.

Erin swore. It sounded funny, her little voice in all of that empty space, swearing. As if there were someone to hear her or care. Nobody was there. Nobody cared what happened to her.

The only person who cared what happened wanted her to die.

Erin couldn't think of any other reason she would be tied up and left in a dark cave with no equipment. Someone wanted to kill her.

Not a person like William Andrews, who did things with his hands. Someone who didn't want to stab or shoot or throttle her. The kind of person who would rather just stand by and watch her die. Or leave her there without waiting to see how long it took.

The kind of person who had taken Angela's autoinjector and left her there to choke to death in the cool basement of the bakery.

Erin's brain moved creakily. Each thought and deduction was an effort of will, not the effortless flow that she normally experienced.

Not Vic. It hadn't been Vic who had killed Angela. It wasn't Vic's voice she could remember hearing. Someone else.

Erin groaned.

Every time she awoke, she had to remember again. She had to force herself to remember where she was and why, and to try to sort out who had done this to her and how she was going to get out of it. And by the time she could get that far, she had started to fade again, her body and her brain in too advanced a state of shock to do anything about it.

She tried to raise her head. It was excruciating.

There was a fine balance between forcing herself to move in order to wake up and pushing herself so hard that she blacked out again. She had to move only a fraction of an inch at a time, then wait for the pain to subside to a more bearable level, and then make another infinitesimal movement.

She swore again, with the pain this time.

She wasn't going to save herself lying on the hard ground trying to make sense of what had happened to her. It didn't matter whether or not she could solve Angela's murder and figure out who had hurt her and left her there to die.

What mattered was moving. Finding some way to get herself out of there. Underground, she was just going to freeze to death. Shock would kill her. Or the swelling of her brain inside her skull. Was that what was making it difficult to breathe?

She had raised her head just enough to know that she still couldn't see anything. And as long as she was lying on her back, she was not going to be able to move. She needed to change her orientation, not just move her head.

Easier said than done.

She felt a little more awake and alert with her head raised. But moving her whole body was going to take a lot of work.

Her hands and her feet were each tied together, but she was not hog-tied. And her hands were tied in front of her body, not behind. That meant it was conceivable that she could crawl, hitching forward on hands and knees, if she could slither onto her belly.

Conceivable, but maybe not possible.

She tried to turn over, but her body didn't follow the instructions from her mind.

Erin stretched her arms out in front of her, then let them drop slowly to the side, trying to use the pull of gravity to help inch her body over. Her shoulder lifted off of the rocky ground, but she needed more.

She'd participated in yoga and workout classes before. How many times had she performed boat pose without worrying about anything but how long she could keep her core tight and hold the pose without shaking? She'd never had to worry that she was going to pass out and let her head go crashing back to the solid rock beneath her. She'd never had to worry that her arms and legs wouldn't both obey her brain's instructions at the same time.

And her legs and arms had never been so heavy.

They didn't feel like her own arms and legs. They felt like they were tied, not just to each other, but to the ground. Pressing one shoulder into the ground, Erin managed to get her conjoined legs up off the ground, and then shifted them to allow them to lower to the ground, turning her body in the process.

She was sweating when she was finally lying on her side instead of on her back. Sweating, clammy, and shivering all at the same time.

Erin tried to control her breathing. She didn't like the raspy noise that was coming out of her. Her head was spinning again with the new orientation and she just wanted to put her head down and rest.

But she was afraid that if she did so, she would pass out again. And maybe she wouldn't wake back up. She needed to move.

Erin held her hands in front of her chest and tried to maneuver one leg around and to twist her body onto her belly. It took a few tries, ages and ages. But she was still awake and finally in a position to move away from the spot she'd been lying in. How long had she been there? Minutes or hours? Or days? There was no way to measure the passage of time.

She had pictured herself crawling on hands and knees. But the reality wasn't so pretty or well-coordinated. She was more like an inchworm or like a baby commando crawling. Unsteadily. She couldn't move her arms and legs in tandem. She couldn't get right up on her knees and elbows. She could just inch and squirm forward, listening to her breath rasp in the pitch blackness.

Erin had never seen such darkness before. It wasn't just the lack of moon or stars or any visible shapes around her. It was as if the world had ceased to exist at all. There were no shades of light or dark. It was as if her vision had been completely taken away from her. And with a head injury, that wasn't beyond the realm of possibility. Perhaps something in her eyes or brain had been damaged beyond repair.

She didn't know whether she could call it progress. She stayed against the wall, using it as a guide to keep her going in a straight line. She kept bumping into it with her body or shoulder, trying as hard as she could to keep from banging her head into it. If she banged her head, she wasn't sure she would ever wake up again.

It wasn't Vic. It wasn't Vic. The mantra kept running through her head as she wriggled and inched along.

Then where was Vic? Was she lying there somewhere in the darkness too? Erin couldn't hear Vic breathing. Did that mean she was dead, or in another cave? Or had she become separated from Erin and was looking for her? Or had she gone back to get help?

What if Vic were more badly hurt than Erin was and needed her help?

She had to keep pushing herself. No matter how exhausting it was and how impossible it seemed. She didn't know whether she had one hundred feet or several miles to crawl before she got out of the cave. She didn't know in what direction safety lay, but she put that out of her mind and just kept moving. If she stopped, she wouldn't get anywhere.

Then suddenly, there was nothing in front of her.

Chapter Fifteen

ERIN'S ARMS DANGLED IN empty air and she took all of her weight suddenly on her chest and stomach, nearly knocking the wind out of her. She froze.

She swore.

She only had to move backward a bit. Readjust her direction and crawl along the edge of the precipice until she reached another wall. Or another precipice. Eventually, she would find solid ground that led away from the cliff edge.

For a few minutes, she lowered her head and tried to fight off the tears and fatigue.

She didn't have the time to feel sorry for herself. She didn't know how long it would be before her body succumbed to the shock or the concussion. She might have only minutes before her time was up. And Vic might need her.

It might be too late for both of them, but Erin had to believe that there was still some chance of survival. She couldn't just give up and let her life trickle away into nothingness. She hadn't had an easy life, but she wasn't ready for it to end. Not when she had just started up a new business. And made new friends.

And she had a cat.

What would happen to Orange Blossom if she never returned home? There was no shelter, just the vet, who would give the cat a few days and then put him to sleep. Erin couldn't let that happen.

She crawled along the edge of the cliff, terrified she was going to overbalance and roll over it. She kept her body as flat to the ground as she could.

"Vic?" Would her voice carry all the way down to the bottom, if Vic had fallen or slid over that edge? How far down was it? A few feet or hundreds? "Vic, are you there?"

There was still no answer. Her voice sounded lost in the darkness, reaching far out before it was stopped by the walls of the cavern.

"Why did we have to go caving?" Erin muttered, as she squirmed along. "Spelunking, then. *It'll be fun, Erin.*" She affected a falsetto. "*It'll be an adventure.* Adventure, my foot! I could live without an adventure like this!"

She stopped for a moment to get her breath back. She could barely move an inch at a time and her breath was as labored as if she'd been sprinting. Another inch or two and she had reached another wall. Erin turned, following the wall, leaving the precipice behind her.

Erin muttered to herself, "Remind me never to go in another cave again."

She realized she had passed out again. How long this time? With no way to tell the time, she felt like it had been days. When had she last eaten? Her lips were cracked and her tongue swollen.

And when had she actually slept, rather than just passing out where she lay? She was worried she didn't have much time left.

It was so easy.

Erin heard the words as clear as a bell. Like the woman was still right there beside her.

You thought you were so clever, with all your ideas and questions. You could outsmart the police department and the killer. You could figure it all out on your own. No one would even know you were investigating it, with your innocuous little questions. Just getting to know people in Bald Eagle Falls. Just making friends and getting to know people.

And Erin couldn't really deny it was true. She had thought that if she just gave it a little time and engaged people, she could eventually sort out who it was that had killed Angela.

She had been naive. She obviously watched too many TV sleuths or read too many mystery books. It was always so easy in the fictional world. But she'd gotten too close to exposing the killer without even realizing what it was she knew. That never happened to Miss Marple.

Erin wiggled along. Her brain felt like it was sloshing around inside her head like a seasick turtle. Every movement brought pain. She thought she would get used to it, or it would subside once she got moving, but she was wrong. She hadn't thought it could feel any worse, but it could.

Seeing us together and then letting me know you intended to blackmail me. All the while pretending to be the sweet little baker. You know I actually felt bad when Terry Piper suspected you? I never thought he would pin it on you. And if you'd just left well enough alone, the case would have gone cold. He never would have had enough to arrest you. It wasn't like he wanted to.

The knot on the back of her head gave one particularly sharp, all-consuming throb and Erin's stomach erupted. She didn't know when she had last eaten, but apparently that didn't matter. The retching made the pain worse and the pain made the retching worse. She stayed there, frozen, trying to keep her body turned in such as way that she wouldn't drench herself with the vomit or end up having to squirm through the puddle. The acid sharp smell of bile filled her nose and she didn't suppose she'd managed to avoid getting it all down her shirt. She was already soaking wet with cold sweat from the effort of crawling along the floor.

She wanted nothing so much as to just lie down and rest.

But after the retching stopped, she forced herself to continue onward. She wouldn't get anywhere if she didn't move.

Blackmail? She hadn't threatened to blackmail anyone. Angela was the one who had been the blackmailer. She was the one who had hoarded all their secrets.

Had Mary Lou been lying when she said she had no secrets? Everybody had something to hide. Was she really the exception?

She had good reason to hate Angela, whether she had any secrets or not.

Gema? She seemed open and friendly, but appearances could be deceiving. If everyone had secrets, that meant that Gema did too. She hadn't invested with Angela, hadn't lost everything she ever had. But that didn't mean that she didn't have anything to hide.

Or was it Melissa? Had Melissa the gossip accidentally said something to Angela that she shouldn't? Or had her involvement with Trenton been less innocent than she had let on? Maybe she had been involved in Trenton's disappearance. Or maybe she knew something about it, something that Angela had done. Had she confronted Angela? Had she just been unable to hold back her hate for the family another minute?

Why had any of them waited? They had all known Angela for years. And yet, something had changed recently. Something had triggered Angela's murder.

Erin breathed hard, swallowed, and breathed some more. It felt like she had been crawling for hours. The darkness obscured any landmarks and she could not see how far she had gone. A few feet? Had she made headway down a long corridor, or was she still only inches from where she had started, traveling in a U shape when she hit the precipice and ended up turning back the way she had come?

What was it about blackmail? Her attacker had said that Erin had tried to blackmail her. What had Erin discovered that was a secret from the rest of the town? How could she blackmail anyone? All that she knew she had been told by other townspeople.

Erin's mind was circling feverishly. She wasn't able to stay focused on the killer's words and sort them out. Instead, her mind went back to opening day. She tried to count each of the patrons who had come through the store to keep herself alert. The Fosters. The older couple who had taken so long to make their choice. The church ladies. Angela. There had been businessmen and other women from the town. Not Officer Piper, he hadn't come until later.

She should have listened to him and just let him investigate. She had been stupid to try to draw the killer out, asking questions about keys and blathering on about hidden treasure. Who would ever believe such a story?

Melissa had. The poor woman seemed to believe every story she was told hook, line, and sinker. Ghosts, Confederate treasure, everything. Or had it been Mary Lou? Pretending to be skeptical, but checking just to be sure.

"Just a little further," Erin said aloud. She didn't know how far it was. But she could feel how she was lagging. How her body was gradually shutting down, one muscle fiber at a time, until she would no longer be able to push and pull her body forward.

She had to believe that she had some chance of getting out.

Time stretched on. It seemed as if Erin had been crawling all night. Crawling for days, even. In spite of the numbness in her fingers and toes, she could still feel all of the exposed skin being scraped away. And her head continued to roil and throb with every movement. Still, she pushed on.

There was a noise far off in the distance.

At first, she thought it was just her brain. The murderer talking to her again in her brain.

Erin. Erin poking her nose into everything. Can't leave well enough alone. Erin. Erin.

But then Erin realized it wasn't the killer's voice. Someone *was* calling her name.

It was so faint that she could only hear it clearly when she held her breath. They were so far away, she knew they wouldn't be able to hear her weak voice if she tried to answer. Best to conserve what little voice she had left for when they got closer. And in the meantime, to try to get closer.

It was a male voice. Or several voices. She couldn't tell whether the overlapping words were separate voices or echoes.

But someone was there looking for her.

Someone would find her and help her, if she could just get close enough for him to find her.

She was so eager to reach the voices that she forgot to take care, and smashed her face into an outcropping rock.

Erin let out a yelp of pain and sucked in her breath over her teeth, trying to breathe through it and keep the pain under control.

Once steadied, she tried to feel in front of her with her hands. There as a wall in front of her. Not just a single outcropping. Erin searched for a hole, for a break, but there was none. How had she gotten into the cave if it was blocked on every side? Erin turned, following the wall around. She was crawling away from the voices, but was determined to get turned around again as soon as she could. The caves were a maze. But if she could just keep following the wall, keep it to her right, that was the way to get out of a labyrinth, wasn't it?

A fraction of an inch at a time. She didn't know how long it would take to get around the wall and facing the right direction again. Or maybe she never would. Maybe they'd just keep missing each other in the dark, moving along parallel tunnels, never meeting up.

"Hello?" Erin tried to call out. "Vic?"

It wasn't Vic looking for her. She knew that. But she was still missing the girl, hoping that she was okay, not lying dead in the darkness somewhere close by.

"Erin?"

The voices were still too far away. They couldn't hear her.

Erin's body shuddered. She was getting too weak. Too cold and weak to continue. Her traitorous body was getting ready to shut down.

"No. No, no, no. Keep going. Keep moving."

Then she spotted the twinkle of a light. At first, she thought it was just an image from her brain. Maybe that light that people claimed to see when they had near-death experiences. The scientists she had read about said they were just images thrown up by the oxygen-starved brain. They weren't really anything. Just hallucinations.

But she stayed focused on it and kept squirming toward it. She didn't care if it was a hallucination or not, it was a goal. And she sorely needed a goal to work toward.

"You see?" she told herself aloud. "Hang in there just a bit longer. I can get us out of here."

The light was getting bigger and brighter. Not very quickly, but it was definitely a light and not just a hallucination. It was more than just a twinkle or a flash.

Then it was gone. It just winked out and disappeared.

"No!" Erin shouted. "No, don't go!"

The words were so forceful they ripped her dry, raw throat. She heard them echo off of the hard stone walls. It didn't sound like her voice, but it was louder than any sound she had been able to make up until then.

A few more seconds passed in blackness and then the light reappeared.

"Yes," Erin whispered.

"Erin?" The searcher's voice was stronger now too, getting closer. "Erin, are you there? I'm coming."

"Yes."

Her brain was telling her that it was okay to stop and rest. Help was on the way and she could just wait for it. But she was afraid that if she stopped, her shocked body was going to shut down completely. It would be too late for them to do anything for her.

"You can't stop now," she said sternly. "You have to keep going. Keep pushing."

And she did. Each excruciating, infinitesimal inch at a time. Her hands and face and knees raw. Her head nauseated, alternating throbbing with a sharp, stabbing pain.

Something was approaching her in the darkness. The light hadn't yet reached her, it was still somewhere in the distance. A mile away? Closer? Farther? It was impossible to tell. But there was definitely something moving toward her, low to the ground, not a human footstep but some kind of animal.

"No! Get out of here!" Erin whispered sharply. She was too weak to defend herself from a predator. And so close to being found and rescued...! She puckered her lips and whistled, as high and loud as she could, trying to scare the creature away. Rat or coyote or whatever it was, surely it wouldn't like the unexpected noise. It would know that she wasn't yet weak enough to be taken.

"Erin?" came the distant call from the bobbing light.

The creature came at her then. But it wasn't growling or snarling. And when it approached, it didn't bite her. There was no attack.

It let out a bark.

Erin's brain scrambled to sort out the new information. A bark? A dog? It wasn't trying to avoid her rescuer, but to call him.

"K9?"

He nosed at her. He gave a little whine, snuffling and investigating. She couldn't take a full-on doggie greeting and was thankful he didn't jump on her or try to join in with this new, unfamiliar game. Instead, he lay down beside her, settling his long, warm body beside her torso. He barked again, a single time, encouraging the searcher to hurry up.

Erin stopped trying to crawl. She relaxed her body, melting into K9, trying to soak up his body's warmth.

The light was close enough that she could detect the dip of each individual step. Erin was breathing heavily through her mouth.

"Erin!" The man's pace redoubled. He must have been able to make something out in the darkness. Erin still couldn't see him, hidden in the darkness behind the light.

Then he was right there in front of her, the light shining full in Erin's face. Her eyes streamed and she couldn't open them.

Piper was swearing, the light moving around as he examined her without touching her. He clicked a walkie-talkie.

"She's here. We're going to need the stretcher."

There was a staticky, garbled response. The man was leaning over her.

"Erin, can you hear me?"

She avoided nodding. Moving her head would just make the pain and nausea worse.

"Yes," she whispered.

He swore again. "You're a mess. What can I do?"

Erin rasped for breath. "Air?"

"Yes. Yes, I have oxygen." He went to work. There was a thud and a clank as he put down his gear. Zippers buzzing and equipment being shifted around. "Can I turn you onto your back?"

"Okay... might pass out... hit on the head."

He bent close to examine her head and swore.

"I see it. I'll put a pad over it and try to cushion it."

He worked to secure a bandage over the bump without much success.

"That's not going to work," he said finally. He put a mask over her mouth and carefully worked the elastic around behind her head, doing his best to avoid the worst of the damage. He put something on the stone floor beneath her. Not a blanket. Maybe a balled-up rain poncho. "You can rest on that."

Erin lowered her head a hair's breadth at a time until her cheek was resting on the squeaky vinyl pillow. Piper checked the oxygen mask and opened the release valve on the small oxygen tank.

"That should help."

Erin tried to relax. She was safe now. Piper would get her out of the cave. They would tend to all her injuries. They would warm her up again.

Piper pulled out an emergency blanket, unfolded it, and laid it over her. His fingers found her wrist and stayed there for a minute, monitoring her pulse.

"Vic?" Erin asked. "Where's Vic?"

"What?"

Her voice was muffled by the oxygen mask. Erin tried to make her words as clear as possible. "Where... is... Vic?"

"Vic is fine."

"She's okay?"

"Yes. She came to get help. She did the right thing."

Erin sighed in relief. She waited for unconsciousness to take her away, but it didn't. She lay still there, listening to her own breathing. She was thankful for the heat of K9's body. He still lay against her, warming her up directly and heating the air trapped under the reflective blanket.

"Who was it?" Erin asked.

The light turned toward her. "You don't know?"

"I don't remember... I heard her voice..."

"Well, best if I don't tell you anything yet. I don't want to taint your testimony."

Erin thought about that. He was probably right.

She felt like she was floating up above them. The pain in her head wasn't going away. If anything, it was getting worse. She hoped that she could last until they got a stretcher in there and got her out. Was it far? It seemed like a long time since Piper had radioed that he wanted a stretcher.

He would feel so bad if he couldn't even get Erin out of the cave alive. She really didn't want to do that to him.

"Erin." There was a little nudge on her arm. "Erin, are you okay?"

Erin tried to rouse herself.

"Wha...?"

"Maybe you should keep talking to me. You have a head injury, I don't think I should let you go to sleep."

"Not sleeping."

"You're drifting."

"Uh-huh."

"Why don't you try to tell me what you remember? Do you remember how you got here?"

"No..."

He nudged her again. Erin was able to blink now and squint at him when his light wasn't shining right in her face. It was nice to be able to see again. She hadn't been blind after all. Just in total darkness.

"You're drifting again. Can you keep your eyes open?"

"Keep the light away."

"Oh. Sorry." He readjusted the headlamp so that it was pointing up instead of down at Erin. "There. How's that?"

"Better."

"What's the last thing you remember?"

Erin took a few deep breaths of the oxygen, hoping it would clear her muddled brain.

"Remember the tea."

"What tea?"

"At the bakery. After church."

"You went to church?" His tone was one of surprise.

"No. The ladies. The church ladies came... for tea. To Auntie Clem's."

"After *they* went to church."

"Yes."

"I didn't think you were a churchgoer."

"No." She wondered briefly what she had said or done that had clued him in to the fact. Or maybe he had just heard gossip around town. It did seem to be a little scandalous, the type of thing people loved to share around. In a Bible-belt town like Bald Eagle Falls, someone openly admitting to being an atheist was shocking.

"I'll let you in on a little secret." He leaned forward. His voice was low and confidential. She couldn't see more than the shadows of his face and had to picture the dimple in his cheek.

"What?"

"I'm not either."

"A Christian?"

"Well... I was raised Christian... so I guess I still am. But I don't go to church."

"Why not?"

"I say it's because of my work schedule. People are very understanding; they know emergency services still have to protect the public on Sundays."

"But...?"

"But... that's not why."

She waited for him to say more, but he didn't explain further.

"So, you had the church ladies over to the bakery for tea after their services? Clementine used to do that, didn't she?"

"Yes."

"I'll bet they all enjoyed that. Everything went off well? Without a hitch?"

"Yes." Erin's voice was tired and far away.

"Nothing that seemed... out of place? Or that indicated you were in any danger?"

"No. Nothing like that."

"You didn't feel threatened?"

"No."

There was a dragging noise, starting in the distance but getting gradually closer. Erin saw another light, twinkling off in the distance. Piper sighed.

"That will be the stretcher. Then we can get you out of this hole and to the hospital for proper care."

"Yeah. Good."

They were silent for a while, both watching and listening to the man approaching with the stretcher. It wasn't a wheeled gurney, which wouldn't have been able to roll over the uneven floor, but a stretcher that had to be carried between two people and was currently being dragged behind one.

Piper turned to look at the newcomer and the man's face was lit up by Piper's headlamp.

"Oh. It's *you.*"

William Andrews looked down at Erin. His face, blackened as always, seemed both amused and concerned.

"We haven't exactly been introduced. My name is Willie. William Andrews."

"Hi," Erin greeted faintly. She looked at Piper, concerned. Hadn't he heard the rumors of William Andrews's supposed drug-running? What was he doing there?

Was Erin in one of his caves? One of the caves that Gema had said to stay away from? Had they gone straight to the caves that Gema had advised them to avoid?

"Mr. Andrews is something of an expert on the caves in the area," Piper said. "When I needed a guide to help me find you, I knew he was the one person I could trust."

Unless William Andrews had been somehow involved in Angela's murder. Or Erin's attack. Or drug-running and stashing drugs in remote caves where they could be hidden from prying eyes. Erin's heart sped and her breaths started to come in gasps again.

Piper put a hand on Erin's shoulder. It was very warm and had a much stronger calming effect than she would have expected. "Trust me," he said softly. And Erin did.

William Andrews put the stretcher down and he and Piper moved in concert to lay it down next to Erin. Once it was in place, Piper shooed K9 out of the way.

"Sorry, boy, can't carry you too!"

K9 obediently moved off to the side and waited.

"Do you think you have any back or neck injuries?" Piper asked. "Obviously, you have a head injury, and that could mean a neck injury as well. Do you have any numbness or tingling? Pain in your back?"

"Numb from the cold," Erin said.

William Andrews shone his headlamp along the floor of the passage, following Erin's trail. "She's already been moving around. I think we're fine lifting her onto the stretcher. It's less than she's done by herself already."

He walked a few feet along the passageway, then returned to Erin and Piper.

"We need to move her to get her out of here. We don't have a back board or collar. We can't wait for them to deploy a rescue team from Chattanooga; she's already in shock."

Piper nodded his agreement.

"I concur. Erin, do you want us to move you? Or call for help?"

"You do it."

"Okay. I want you to try to stay completely still. We'll do this as gently as we can, but it may still hurt."

"I know."

The two men got into position. Erin took a couple of deep breaths to try to calm and relax herself and prepare for the jolt she was going to get.

When she awoke, it took some time to swim through the fog of her brain and sort out the sensations. She was still face-down and still tied up. She was moving, rolling up and down or back and forth, she wasn't sure of the axis. Just the movement, like a ship rolling over waves on the ocean. It made her seasick, the nausea building up inside her.

She choked, trying not to vomit, but she knew she wouldn't be able to hold it back. The movement stopped and she was set down on a hard surface. Someone was holding her head, turning it to the side as she threw up again, foul, acidic bile burning her throat and nose.

Erin was pretty sure she had baptized her assistant. She realized she was no longer wearing the oxygen mask. Maybe it wasn't the first time she had thrown up. Or maybe it had been too awkward to keep the mask on her while she was on the stretcher.

"Okay?" he questioned.

In the light that moved around her, Erin saw that it was Piper. Officer Piper had rescued her. Was rescuing her. Soon they would be out of the darkness, able to see the light of day once more.

"Yeah. Thanks."

"You done?"

"Seasick."

He chuckled. "Sorry about that. We'll do our best to make it a smooth ride."

They again lifted the stretcher and resumed their walk down the twisting paths of the caves. Erin tried to focus her eyes on something to combat the nausea, but they were still surrounded by darkness. The light from the men's helmets was enough to illuminate the space for a few feet, but the little bubble of light didn't extend very far.

She tried to focus instead on her attacker. Did Piper already know who it was, or was he expecting her to supply the details? If Vic had gone to get help, then she must have been able to tell him something. They would have been at the cave together to explore. Vic had seen Erin attacked and had gone for help.

It was a woman's voice. Not William Andrews's. But she wasn't sure which of the women it belonged to.

Seeing us together and then letting me know you intended to blackmail me.

Who had she seen together? She had certainly never told anyone that she was going to blackmail them. The woman had killed Angela for threatening to reveal her secret. And she thought Erin knew and was doing the same thing. She was paranoid about having her secret revealed. That was what had driven her to action both times.

Mary Lou? She claimed to have no secrets. But everybody had secrets. Melissa? Did she know where Trenton was? Did she know what had happened to him, or had she been involved? But that didn't fit the puzzle.

Seeing us together.

The clue was in those three words. Who had she seen together?

"Gema," Erin croaked.

The men heard her and again set down the stretcher so that Piper could talk to Erin face-to-face.

"What was that?" he asked.

"Gema. Was it Gema Reed?"

"What did you remember?" he asked, giving nothing away.

"I'm not sure… it could have been her voice… she said, 'you saw us together.'"

"Who did you see together? What was she talking about?"

"I saw her at the camping store… she said… it was her cousin."

"Her cousin?"

"She was talking to a woman…"

Piper shook his head. "So?"

"I don't know… she said it was her cousin."

"Why wouldn't it be?"

Erin tried to sort it out. She pictured their faces, thought about their expressions and body language as they had been talking together. As cousins, it made sense that they were close. That they were friendly.

If Gema had been upset by Erin seeing them together, though, then maybe she had something to hide and they weren't just cousins.

Erin licked her chapped lips. Both her tongue and her lips were like sandpaper. So dry, they just rasped against each other.

"Do you have water?"

"I do," William Andrews offered, standing close by. He put down his backpack and pulled out a water bottle.

"How long was it?" Erin whispered to Piper.

"How long... were you in here?"

"Yes."

"It's been..." he held his watch close to his eyes and twisted his wrist back and forth, trying to catch the light of his headlamp. "Just over twenty-four hours."

William Andrews crouched beside her, holding the water bottle sideways for Erin to drink from. She ended up with water down her face, trying to drink at such an odd angle, but she was glad to moisten her lips and mouth.

"Thank you."

He nodded. "Let's keep going," he told Piper. "The longer we stop to talk, the worse her condition is going to get."

Erin was impressed with the way William Andrews took over. In town, she had taken him to be an untrained laborer, someone who was only able to get odd jobs because he couldn't hold down anything permanent. But it was obvious from Piper's deference to him on matters caving and medical that there was more to William Andrews than there appeared.

They hoisted her up without any further discussion. Erin still wanted to talk to Officer Piper, to try to sort out the random bits of knowledge knocking around her brain. Somehow, she knew Gema's secret. Gema thought she was a threat.

Was it because of the woman at the store? Or something else?

They seemed to be on an uphill slope. Erin wished they had untied her wrists so that she could hold on to the edges of the stretcher, as she felt her body shifting down toward the end. There was light now, more than just what was coming from the two men's headlamps. Erin lay still and tried to see where it was coming from. It kept brightening the farther they went up. And then Erin was blinking, her eyes streaming, as they broke out of the cave into the light.

There were people there. She wasn't sure who, because the sun cut into her brain like a knife and forced her to squeeze her eyes shut in an effort to block it out. She was afraid she was going to throw up again and called for Piper to help her. They put down the stretcher, but the man who ministered to her was not Officer Piper. He was a doctor or paramedic, barking out orders like an army general.

Erin cowered there, overwhelmed by the noise and the light and the pain. They put a collar around her neck to hold it still and wrapped a bandage around and around her head before laying her down on a backboard. Once she was face-up, they finally cut away the ties that bound her arms and legs.

"I still don't want you to move," the doctor told her gruffly. "I'm going to immobilize your arms and legs. Don't be afraid, it's just to protect your spine until we know the extent of your injuries."

Erin didn't say anything as he proceeded to do so. Tears were streaming from her eyes. While mostly they were from the sun, Erin was also at the end of her rope. Far past the end of her rope, in fact.

"Where's Vic?" she asked, before they loaded her into the ambulance. "Is she okay?"

"I'm here!" It sounded like Vic was calling from far away. "I'm right here, Erin. I'm fine."

"Is she hurt? Vic? Are you hurt?"

"No. I'm okay. Not hurt."

"Good. Did you remember to feed Orange Blossom?"

Vic laughed. "The cat is taken care of, don't you worry! But he cried all night looking for you and kept the neighbors up!"

They slid her into the ambulance, away from the bright sunlight. Away from the crowds of people. "Terry? Is Officer Piper there…?"

"He can meet us at the hospital. Just rest, now."

Despite the layers of bandages wrapped around her head, every bump and bounce of the ambulance caused excruciating pain and made it feel like her brain was bouncing around the inside of her skull. She closed her eyes and tried to do as the doctor told her and rest.

Chapter Sixteen

WITH VIC BESIDE HER, holding her hand, Erin was finally able to relax and believe that her young assistant was safe and well. For so many hours, she had been sure that Vic was lying in the cave somewhere, dead or dying. No matter how many times they told her Vic was okay, she couldn't really believe it until she could see and touch Vic for herself.

"How much do you remember?" Officer Terry Piper inquired, sitting in the other visitor chair observing the two of them.

"Most of it, I think," Erin said. "Some of it is still kind of foggy, but hopefully Vic can fill in those parts."

She glanced at Vic. The pretty blonde nodded.

The painkillers in Erin's IV kept her reasonably comfortable and she didn't have to move around anymore. They had operated, removing a piece of her skull to ease the pressure the swelling had caused, and cleaning up the wound and the fracture Gema had caused.

It was Gema. Erin could remember that much now.

"How did she know where we were going?" Erin asked Vic. "You didn't tell her which cave we were going to, did you?"

"No." Vic shook her head. "She must have guessed. She just told me not to go to the Beaver Creek caves. So that convinced me to go to the old mine."

"She knew we'd go one of those two places?"

"She knew we were beginners, but we didn't want a big commercial outfit. So... that only left a couple of choices nearby. I guess it was a good bet."

"I suppose if we'd gone somewhere else, she would have waited for another opportunity." Erin looked over at Officer Piper. "Seems like she was pretty good at waiting for the right opportunity."

He nodded. "So it would seem." He was being very careful not to tell her any of what he knew, which Erin found annoying. She knew it was the right thing for him to do. He couldn't plant information in her brain. But it was still annoying. She wanted to talk to him about what he knew, not drag the story out of her brain one thread at a time.

"So, we got there, got all our gear out and ready. And then... Vic had to... uh... do something."

"Do what?" Piper asked suspiciously.

"I had to pee!" Vic laughed. "So... I went into the trees to find a private spot..."

"It's not like you had to go far," Erin said. "I could have just turned my back."

Vic shrugged. "I'm shy. I had to be where I knew no one could see me."

"And that's when Gema showed up," Erin explained. "I don't know where she parked her car; I didn't see it. She just came... out of nowhere. She hit me with something before I even saw her."

"I think a shovel," Vic told her.

Erin reached up and touched her bandaged head. "A shovel," she echoed.

"Ouch."

"Yeah. She hit me and I just went over like a log. After that, I'm not sure of much. She tied my hands and feet, I guess, and dragged me into the cave."

"So that when I came back from the woods, Erin was nowhere to be seen," Vic contributed. "I thought maybe she decided to use the facilities before going down as well, so I waited." She looked at Erin. "But you never came back."

"You must have been scared," Erin empathized.

"Me? *You* must have been terrified! That woman dragging you down to the bowels of the earth! You didn't even want to go exploring to begin with. I had to talk you into it. Being down there with your skull caved in and a homicidal woman railing away at you…!"

"It was scary," Erin admitted. "It was so dark. She had a light, but I could barely see anything. She didn't even let me walk, she just dragged me from one place to another. She must be really strong!"

"She used to do lots of exploring and climbing," Piper agreed. "She's quite athletic."

Erin looked back at Vic again. "Do you remember seeing Gema at the camping store?"

"Yes, of course."

"What do you remember about it?"

Vic thought back. "She helped me to pick out a compass. I don't know what else. She told us about Angela and how she had messed things up so badly for Mary Lou, when Mary Lou invested with her."

"Do you remember anything else?"

"Nnno…?"

Erin didn't say anything right away. Vic shook her head, looking bewildered. "What else? What am I missing?"

"She was talking to someone."

"Before she talked to us?" Vic shrugged. "One of the sales clerks."

"Yes."

"What about it?"

"Gema didn't look like she was there looking for something or getting help. She was having a friendly chat with her, not asking for advice."

"Right." Vic nodded her agreement. "And she said something. That she was just checking up on her cousin, or something like that."

"Yes. But when she was talking to me, when she took me down to that cave to leave me there… she said, 'you saw us.' Because I saw the two of them together."

"So, what? Why wouldn't she be talking to her cousin? Who cares if someone saw them together?"

"But she did care. So, it wasn't her cousin. It was somebody she didn't want to be seen with."

"Why not?"

"She'd already been blackmailed by Angela. She'd killed Angela to stop her from revealing Gema's secret. And when I said something, she thought it was starting all over again."

Vic looked puzzled. She shook her head slowly, not believing it.

"What did you say to her?" Officer Piper asked.

"I made a comment about her being there to see someone." Erin looked over at Vic, reminding her. "They'd been having a very close conversation and they hugged goodbye. Gema didn't see us until afterward; she didn't know she'd been seen until then. And then I brought up how Angela knew everyone's secrets and used those secrets to get her own way…"

Piper chuckled. Vic was a little slower to understand; then her face got a little pink.

"She thought you were telling her that you knew her secret now so you were going to blackmail her?"

"Yes. She thought I was just being subtle, in front of you. But I wasn't being subtle… I was completely clueless that I'd just seen her…"

"You think they were *lovers*?"

Erin shook her head. "Good guess, but I don't think so. I didn't think anything of it when she said the girl was her cousin, because they had similar features. So, I'm thinking she wasn't a cousin, but maybe… her daughter."

"But I thought Gema only had boys. Isn't that what she said?"

"That's what she said. *She and Fred* only had boys. She must have had the girl out of wedlock."

"And she went to church with those other Christian women. If they knew she'd had another child…"

"She was willing to kill to keep that secret from them."

"Oh, wow."

"Did she say anything to you about Mrs. Plaint's murder?" Piper inquired.

Erin sighed. She put her fingers over her ears for a minute, as if she could block out the words that kept replaying in her mind.

"She said it was so easy. That's what she kept saying. Angela's allergy made it a piece of cake." Erin laughed humorlessly at her turn of phrase. "Gema went down to the basement. She knew Angela would go down there because… she liked to snoop into other people's business. She'd go down there to have a look around. She'd go up to the kitchen, if the door was left unlocked, have a snoop around there too. But Angela never got that far. Because Gema was waiting for her."

"How would she poison Mrs. Plaint?" Piper asked. "How would she convince Mrs. Plaint to eat something that had been contaminated? I'd be pretty suspicious of someone who laid in wait for me and then offered me food. Especially if I was deathly allergic to something like wheat."

"She didn't convince Angela to eat anything." Erin swallowed her disgust. It was difficult to describe what Gema had told her. Gema had thought that Erin would die in that passageway. She was injured, already drifting in an out of consciousness, bound hand and foot. It wouldn't take her long to die in the cold, rarefied air of the deeper caves. No one would find Erin. She would die of exposure, if not from the head injury. "She was so proud of herself. She just put a little flour in her hand. And when Angela got close, blew it in her face. Angela gasped and breathed it in, straight into her lungs."

"And that is as effective as eating it?" Piper asked.

"Probably more so. She took Angela's purse when she started to react, saying that she would use an autoinjector to save her... and then just stole the autoinjectors. Wiped Angela's face so that she didn't have flour all over it. And walked back out. Left her there to die."

"What a horrible thing to do!" Vic said, outraged.

Erin nodded her head the tiniest bit. "I agree."

Officer Piper was writing notes in his notepad and didn't look up at them for a couple of minutes. Then he became aware of their attention and raised his brows.

"Now will you tell us what happened with Gema?" Erin asked. "Did you arrest her? Did she confess?"

Piper shifted to get more comfortable in his seat, giving Erin a little smile that showed the dimple in his cheek. "Vic was pretty quick about getting help, once she took a closer look around and saw the bloody shovel on the ground. She drove out to the highway and called me as soon as she could get a signal. I scrambled whatever help I could get from Bald Eagle Falls and the city and got out there. Gema was still in the caves when we got there. I arrested her in connection with your assault and kidnapping when she came out... but she wouldn't talk, wouldn't say where you were. Said that we were just mistaken; she was out there to explore just like any other day. If something had happened to you, she had no idea what it was. And the cave system is pretty complex... you can have several parties down there and never run into each other. We couldn't prove what she had done unless we could find you, get you out safely, and get your story."

"But now you can. Because I'm telling you she's the one who hit me and put me down there."

He nodded. "We'll proceed with formal charges. For that and Mrs. Plaint's murder."

"Thank goodness," Vic breathed.

"Thank you," Erin told them. "Without both of you, I don't think I would ever have gotten out of there alive."

"If it wasn't for me, you wouldn't have been there in the first place," Vic said miserably.

"Don't talk like that. If it hadn't been there, it would have been somewhere else. Maybe somewhere that she had to make sure I was dead right off, instead of just leaving me to die, which seems to be her first preference."

"She's got a point," Piper agreed. "As far as my part in this… I credit Willie and K9." The dog raised his head to look at his master, then put it back down when he decided he wasn't being addressed. "Willie knows those caves better than anyone and it was K9's nose that led us to you."

"I was so glad to see him," Erin said. "Or hear him." She was feeling drowsy again. Pleasantly tired though, rather than the crushing fatigue that had made her feel like she was never going to wake up again if she let herself succumb. She closed her eyes. "I thought he was a coyote."

"Well, be glad he wasn't. A coyote would have made short work of you in that condition."

"I am glad."

"I heard you," Piper said. "Just that one time. I took a turn down the wrong passage and I heard you call out."

"Your light disappeared. I was scared."

"Without you shouting, I don't know if we would have found you in time. So you saved yourself too."

"Hmm."

"I prayed that they would find you," Vic confessed.

Erin opened her eyes and looked at her employee. Vic ducked her head and swept her hair back over one shoulder, getting red.

"Well, I did," she said. "I know you don't believe in God, so I'm sorry, I know I probably shouldn't have, but… it was the only thing I could do."

"You can pray about whatever you like," Erin said. "Even if it's me. I would never dream of interfering."

"Okay." Vic scratched her jaw, still looking embarrassed, but giving Erin a smile. "Thanks."

"I thought you and God weren't on good terms, though."

"Well... that doesn't stop him from answering when I call. And I've decided... to give him the benefit of the doubt. Maybe just because people say that he hates me because of something they say is a sin... maybe he doesn't."

Erin shrugged. "You're okay in my book."

"Thanks." Vic looked down again. "I'm going to go look for coffee. Anyone else want one?"

"Sure," Piper agreed. "I could really use something."

Vic looked pleased. She left the room, giving Erin a wink.

After she was gone, Erin looked at Piper. "I guess you must be pretty tired too. You must have been searching for me for hours."

He nodded. "I'll get some sleep before long." He gazed at the door, checking to be sure Vic was gone. "So, your young friend... she seems to be coming to terms with her... transition?"

Erin's jaw dropped. "How long have you known about that?"

"It *is* my job to investigate a suspect's background."

"But you never said... she was so worried about you finding out."

"She obviously didn't want me to know, so I didn't feel the need to mention it. Once I figured out her identity, I knew why her aunt had turned her away. I wasn't sure if you knew..."

"No, not to start with. It took a few days."

They both just looked at each other for a minute.

"Well, she had the luck to find the two people in town who could keep a secret," Piper said. He straightened up and squared his shoulders. "She has to understand, though... she won't be able to keep her past a secret forever. Not here. It's easier for you, because you're from further away. But Vic's from just a couple of towns away. It won't be long before people start to figure it out."

"I know." Erin's eyes were drooping. She wasn't going to be able to stay awake much longer. She blinked, trying to stay awake just a few more minutes. "And for the record, I'm not trying to hide anything about my past. Just... trying to start fresh."

It was a few days before Erin was up to reopening the bakery. Even then, she had to allow Vic to help with more than usual. The girl was happy to have more of a hand in planning the specials and helping to pull them together. Erin needed to rest often. A high stool beside the counter helped her to keep up even when she was sitting, mixing batters and filling cupcake wrappers or forming cookies. When they opened, Erin found one of the wrought iron chairs normally at the customer tables waiting for her behind the register so that she could rest between orders. It wasn't quite tall enough for her to use while using the register and the stool in the kitchen was too tall, but she could at least stop to rest there as she needed to, and Vic could run a few of the orders through the till. Vic was flourishing under the increased responsibilities, looking for all the world like she was the owner of the shop rather than Erin.

"Will you be staying, then?" Mary Lou asked, as Erin rang up her order for a blueberry muffin. "I was worried that with all this business and your injuries, that you would decide Bald Eagle Falls wasn't for you."

Erin leaned against the counter. Was it madness to consider staying after she had been attacked and kidnapped? She had been the suspect in a murder investigation and she had nearly been killed. Was that really the kind of place she wanted to live? She could sell the business and the house and whatever else was of value in Clementine's house, move to another small town where the cost of living wasn't too high and start over.

But she wasn't sure she was ready to do that. She glanced over at Vic, who was watching her for her answer. Erin had an employee to consider, now her friend and housemate. And there was Orange Blossom. From what Erin understood, cats didn't like moving. He could run away at the first opportunity, if she tried to take him somewhere else and start anew.

"No," she said to Mary Lou. "I don't think I'm going anywhere. I like Bald Eagle Falls and Clementine's old shop... it's one of the only places I have any childhood memories of."

Mary Lou nodded, smiling. "I'm glad," she said. "Don't let all of this nastiness scare you off. There really are a lot of nice people here, once you get to know us."

"Besides," Vic contributed. "What are the chances that you would ever get caught in the middle of another murder in a little place like Bald Eagle Falls?"

Epilogue

ERIN TOOK HER TIME locking up.

The lock turned into place with a satisfying snick. All the locks had been replaced and she knew where all the keys were. There was no one squatting there at night and no ghost.

"What are you doing here?"

Officer Piper's question brought her back to the present. She turned to look at him, giving him and K9 a smile.

"Hi. On your rounds?"

"You should be home by now. Your doctor won't like you doing so much on your first day."

Erin was tired after a long day of work, but was still feeling steady on her feet.

"I'm on my way, as you can see. Vic's already gone to get dinner on, so I'm going to eat and hit the sack. If that meets with your approval."

"Are you okay to drive?" He nodded to the Challenger.

"Yes. The doctor said as long as I'm not feeling dizzy or lightheaded, I can drive."

"Okay."

He watched her walk from the door to her car.

"I'm okay, Officer Piper." She assured him, aware that he was watching her gait to make sure that she wasn't impaired by her concussion.

"Terry," he corrected.

A smile tugged at the corners of Erin's mouth. She ducked her head a little, self-conscious. He had called her Erin during the search, but he couldn't very well have called 'Miss Price' for hours on end. It just wasn't done that way.

"Terry. You don't need to worry about me. Thanks to you I'm just fine."

Did you enjoy this book? Reviews and recommendations
are vital to making a book successful.
Please leave a review at your favorite book store or review
site and share it with your friends.

Don't miss the following bonus material:

Read a sneak preview chapter of the next book
Learn more about the author

Preview of

Dairy-Free Death

ORANGE BLOSSOM NO LONGER howled at night, as long as Erin or Vic were around and the cat could snuggle with one of the two young women when they went to bed. Usually with Erin, but sometimes the traitorous feline chose Erin's eighteen-year-old housemate instead, for no discernible reason. Erin would lie awake, waiting for him to come in, and he simply wouldn't come. She would fall asleep eventually, but those were always restless nights. She got up very early to go to the bakery, and it was those mornings that it was hardest and felt like just throwing in the towel and finding some line of work that kept office hours of nine to five, so she could be a normal person instead of a zombie by evening and an early bird chasing down the worm in the morning.

Orange Blossom no longer kept the neighbors awake, but he still knew how to use his voice, and as soon as Erin stepped into the kitchen following her wake-up shower, he would immediately be winding himself around her ankles, meowing chattily, making sure she couldn't forget to feed him.

Vic laughed as she followed Erin and Orange Blossom into the kitchen. She hit the button on the coffee maker while Erin tripped three times over Orange Blossom trying to get to his food bin in the pantry. Victoria's pink flannel jammies were wrinkled and she smelled warmly of sweat. Her hair was as blond as Erin's hair was dark. Erin's hair was not quite black, but as dark a brown as you could get without being black.

"Why does he still act like that?" Vic asked. "Like he's starving to death and you might forget to feed him? I mean, he's been fed every day. It's a routine now. Shouldn't he be settling down about it?"

Despite the facts that there was only ten years between them and Vic topped her by a head, Erin often felt like she was in a parental role to Vic. She emerged from the pantry with her scoop of kibble and filled Orange Blossom's bowl. Her kitten plunged his head into the bowl that was still too big for him, wolfing the food hungrily, making little yipping noises between gulps.

"I don't know, Vic. I assume that sooner or later… he'll at least dial it back a bit. But you have to remember, he's still just a kitten, and he was a starving street cat when I brought him home."

She remembered how hard he had been to catch, how skittish and slippery he had been. No problem with that now. He was always underfoot. And when she did pick him up, he immediately snuggled against her, purring warmly and bumping the top of his head under her chin. No one would ever guess that he'd once been such a frightened stray.

The first cup of coffee was done and Vic handed it to Erin before putting the second pod in.

"You look tired this morning," she offered by way of explanation, since the first cup was almost always for her.

"I didn't sleep very well. Where was that silly cat? In with you?"

"Yes." Vic giggled. "Right under my chin. Kept getting fur up my nose whenever either of us moved."

Erin shook her head and took a sip of the coffee. It was still too hot to drink, so she held it there, smelling the rich, dark comforting scent. The smell itself was almost as good as the caffeine boost. She sighed and put it down on the counter to cool for a few minutes.

"I'd better grab a couple of things for lunch."

They usually had sandwiches for their early, pre-lunchtime-rush meal, a combination of the bakery bread or buns and whatever fixings were in the fridge. And if they wanted more than tomatoes on toast, Erin needed to restock.

Vic picked up her coffee once the machine finished dripping and headed for the bathroom. By the time Erin was ready for her workday, all of her lists prepared, Vic would be dressed for the day and ready to go. The coffee would hold them both over until the first batch of muffins was fresh out of the oven, and then they would take a break to each have one or two before continuing their preparations. Waking up so early and working through the breakfast and lunch rushes, they took their own meals at odd times.

"Book Club day?" Vic asked as she and Erin climbed into the Challenger to buzz over to the bakery. It was only a few blocks from the little green and white house, but they had things to carry and they would be on their feet all day. It was still dark, a couple of hours before dawn.

"Yes," Erin agreed, mentally reviewing her lists for the day. Book Club Day was a big deal for the ladies, but it didn't really change Erin's product line-up. They enjoyed a cookie or two, but she didn't have to do anything special, just make sure there was a variety to choose from. Vic would make up a platter and take it over to The Book Nook next door after lunch. "And I need to do a cake for Peter Foster's birthday. His mom is so excited about being able to order a bakery cake instead of having to make one herself this year. 'Decorated and everything.'" Erin chuckled over how excited Mrs. Foster had been about it. "She's got her hands full with that little Traci. I honestly don't know how she gets anything done."

"What kind did Peter want?"

"Chocolate cake. Darth Vader. I have a pattern."

"That will be cool." Vic swept her blond hair over her shoulder and tucked stray strands behind her ears. "I wonder what Traci will want on her birthday."

"Anything she can get her hands—and mouth—on."

"I love the way she gets so excited whenever the Fosters come into the shop. When we started, she was just a nursing baby. Now, she wants her cook-kie!"

"Yes, she does!"

As she opened the back door to the bakery and stepped into the kitchen, Erin took a deep breath of the warm, yeasty air. It was like a drug. Or a perfume. Bottle that smell and she would have a better mate-catcher than any floral concoction. The caffeine of her morning coffee was kicking in, and Erin felt energized and excited to begin her day. She always felt like that. It was hard to wake up initially, but by the time she got to the bakery, she was raring and ready to go.

"You want to start with those maple-bacon muffins?" her young assistant suggested.

Vic had initially been disgusted by the idea, but once she tasted the perfect balance of sweet maple and salty, smokey bacon, she was a convert. Now they were one of her favorite, and were frequently her choice for breakfast.

"Sure," Erin agreed. "Maple-bacon it is."

They already had several batters mixed ahead of time, so Erin selected the maple-bacon muffins and put them on the counter while the oven preheated.

~ ~ ~

Dairy-Free Death, Book 2 of Auntie Clem's Bakery Series by P.D. Workman is available now!

About the Author

For as long as P.D. Workman can remember, the blank page has held an incredible allure. After a number of false starts, she finally wrote her first complete novel at the age of twelve. It was full of fantastic ideas. It was the spring board for many stories over the next few years. Then, forty-some novels later, P.D. Workman finally decided to start publishing. Lots more are on the way!

P.D. Workman is a devout wife and a mother of one, born and raised in Alberta, Canada. She is a homeschooler and an Executive Assistant. She has a passion for art and nature, creative cooking for special diets, and running. She loves to read, to listen to audio books, and to share books out loud with her family. She is a technology geek with a love for all kinds of gadgets and tools to make her writing and work easier and more fun. In person, she is far less well-spoken than on the written page and tends to be shy and reserved with all but those closest to her.

~ ~ ~

Please visit P.D. Workman at pdworkman.com to see what else she is working on, to join her mailing list, and to link to her social networks.

~ ~ ~

If you enjoyed this book, please take the time to recommend it to other purchasers with a review or star rating and share it with your friends!

CPSIA information can be obtained
at www.ICGtesting.com
Printed in the USA
FSHW012021271220
77198FS